BAD CALL

Fargo spotted a blur of movement a hundred yards out—a Comanche brave in buckskins and knee-length moccasins, sneaking across sand almost the same color as his clothing. A claybank pony was tethered in a swale behind him. Fargo guessed the short rifle in his hand was a stolen Mexican Army carbine.

Fargo rarely struck without giving a man a fighting chance. He levered a round into the Henry's chamber, hoping these bullets were sound. Then he stood up atop the highest rock, fully exposed to the Comanche below.

The brave froze in place for a full minute, deciding what to do.

"Your call, John," Fargo said in a patient whisper. "Stick or quit."

The Comanche decided to stick. In seconds the carbine was braced in his shoulder socket and he was peppering Fargo's position with lead. . . .

THE
TRAILSMAN
#292

SAN
FRANCISCO
SHOWDOWN

by

Jon Sharpe

A SIGNET BOOK

SIGNET
Published by New American Library, a division of
Penguin Group (USA) Inc., 375 Hudson Street,
New York, New York 10014, USA
Penguin Group (Canada), 90 Eglinton Avenue East, Suite 700, Toronto,
Ontario M4P 2Y3, Canada (a division of Pearson Penguin Canada Inc.)
Penguin Books Ltd., 80 Strand, London WC2R 0RL, England
Penguin Ireland, 25 St. Stephen's Green, Dublin 2,
Ireland (a division of Penguin Books Ltd.)
Penguin Group (Australia), 250 Camberwell Road, Camberwell, Victoria 3124,
Australia (a division of Pearson Australia Group Pty. Ltd.)
Penguin Books India Pvt. Ltd., 11 Community Centre, Panchsheel Park,
New Delhi - 110 017, India
Penguin Group (NZ), cnr Airborne and Rosedale Roads, Albany,
Auckland 1310, New Zealand (a division of Pearson New Zealand Ltd.)
Penguin Books (South Africa) (Pty.) Ltd., 24 Sturdee Avenue,
Rosebank, Johannesburg 2196, South Africa

Penguin Books Ltd., Registered Offices:
80 Strand, London WC2R 0RL, England

First published by Signet, an imprint of New American Library,
a division of Penguin Group (USA) Inc.

First Printing, February 2006
10 9 8 7 6 5 4 3 2 1

The first chapter of this book previously appeared in *The Cutting Kind*, the two
hundred ninety-first volume in this series.

The Trailsman

Beginnings . . . they bend the tree and they mark the man. Skye Fargo was born when he was eighteen. Terror was his midwife, vengeance his first cry. Killing spawned Skye Fargo, ruthless, cold-blooded murder. Out of the acrid smoke of gunpowder still hanging in the air, he rose, cried out a promise never forgotten.

The Trailsman they began to call him all across the West: searcher, scout, hunter, the man who could see where others only looked, his skills for hire but not his soul, the man who lived each day to the fullest, yet trailed each tomorrow. Skye Fargo, the Trailsman, the seeker who could take the wildness of a land and the wanting of a woman and make them his own.

California, 1858—
where the land of gold runs red with blood,
and Skye Fargo is marked for hard death.

1

Many hard trails, and many rough scrapes, had taught Skye Fargo that sudden danger often left a warning tingle in the air. Right now he and his pinto stallion felt it simultaneously.

"Easy, old campaigner," Fargo urged the nervous Ovaro, patting his neck to calm him. "Hell, you know trouble never leaves us alone for long."

The tall, crop-bearded, buckskin-clad rider reined in among some sand dunes and wind-twisted Joshua trees. At first the Trailsman's lake blue eyes, closed to slits against a grueling sun, detected nothing that didn't belong to the area.

He was traversing the vast desert just east of the Mormon settlement of San Bernardino, California. As far as the eye could see was only stark desert brown.

"There's room out here to swing a cat in, all right," Fargo remarked softly, mostly so his voice would calm his sidestepping mount. "Wide open with no good place to mount an ambush. And I don't see any trouble brewing."

The Ovaro nickered, sternly disagreeing with his master.

"I trust your nose better than my eyes." Fargo surrendered, sliding his brass-framed Henry rifle from its saddle boot. He levered a round into the chamber.

Despite the endless risks, once again Fargo's needle pointed west—always west. Following the urge to push over the next ridge, he'd come nearly as far west as a man could get without swimming in the Pacific, this time with lucrative trail work waiting for him the moment he reached a dusty little pueblo just north of Los Angeles. The preferred route to California was the well-established westward trail from Saint Joseph, Missouri. Fargo had followed it at first, counting as many as seventeen pioneer graves to the mile.

Then, tired of the traffic and the ruined water holes, he had opted for the less popular route through the old Spanish land-grant country of the Southwest. He had found little growth besides scrub cottonwood and mesquite. Even so, the route somehow grew more desolate as he followed the Gila River of southern Arizona Territory. Bone-dry expanses of salt sage produced alkali dust, galling his eyes to tears and rawing his throat like harsh tobacco.

Ever since crossing the Colorado River into southeastern California, however, water had become Fargo's chief concern. The vast Lake Cahuilla was too saline, but luckily he had come across the occasional saguaro cactus just bulging with water.

Now, spotting dust puffs beyond the next line of wind-sculpted, rippled dunes, Fargo suspected he had bigger problems than a parched throat.

"Looks like you were right, old warhorse," Fargo told his stallion. "I'm too tired to run, so let's take it by the horns."

He thumped the Ovaro's ribs with his boot heels, holding his Henry straight up with the butt plate resting on his thigh.

Fargo rarely consulted a calendar or timepiece. He reckoned it was somewhere in early fall, cool down on the coastal plain and cold up in the mountains at night. But this daytime desert sun had weight as well as fierce heat. He felt it on his shoulders and back now as he crossed a landscape sparsely dotted with prickly pear, creosote, and cholla.

A female voice jolted Fargo like a slap.

"Newt! Newt, look! Those men are charging at *us,* and their guns are—*oh*!"

The whip-crack sound of a rifle cut her short. Fargo, his vision blocked by the line of dunes, smacked the Ovaro's rump hard.

"No, Newt!" the woman's voice cried next while the Ovaro tried gamely to reach a gallop in deep and sloping sand. "God, no, they'll kill you!"

More gunshots, rifle and pistol, hammered Fargo's ears. Damn sure *sounded* like killing was imminent, he decided.

With the Ovaro making poor time up the steep, almost liquid surface of the dunes, Fargo figured he'd best send in his card, and quick.

He swung the Henry's stock up into his shoulder socket. Unexpected gunshots might take some vinegar out of those attackers, whoever they were. Vicious road gangs, sometimes Mexican, were common in lower California. But Fargo had never heard of them preferring the merciless desert with its scant traffic.

He pulled the Henry's trigger and the hammer clicked uselessly.

Just ahead and out of sight, a conveyance of some sort was trying to gain speed—Fargo could hear iron tires scraping the desert hardpan. The gunfire was an unrelenting crackle now. The woman screamed.

Cursing the Henry's hang fire, Fargo cleared the faulty bullet, jacked a new one into the chamber, and heard the firing pin again click uselessly.

This time Fargo swore with real heat, making up a few words of his own. The ammunition of his day was notoriously unreliable, especially the new self-contained cartridges. He'd found that as many as half the bullets in any given box might malfunction. That was definitely a deterrent to spontaneous showdowns—but left a man vulnerable at times like this.

More gunfire, more female screams, and Fargo's Colt was to hand when he and the Ovaro finally crested the line of dunes.

"Newt! Oh, good heart of God! We're stuck in the sand—*oh*!"

The woman flinched hard when a bullet knocked a chunk off the seat of their rugged Dougherty wagon, a passenger conveyance favored for its strong steel springs. Fargo saw only a young couple in the wagon: the woman and a man in a plug hat and clergy-black suit. He was aiming a long Jennings rifle at four riders, who were bearing down on them with guns blazing. He, too, seemed to be having rifle troubles.

Fargo never fooled himself—with only his Colt, he could never defeat four mounted men armed with repeating rifles. Then again, he reasoned, very few of these California bullyboys had much stomach for a hard fight.

A bullet sent the woman's bonnet twirling even as Fargo, bracing himself against a bag of oats tied to his cantle, shot the front rider's horse out from under him.

The sorrel gelding dropped like a sash weight, trapping the surprised rider's legs. Fargo, loathe to hurt a horse, realized those two travelers had only one chance, and that was if he could put all four attackers on foot, quick. Especially since it was clear the man in the wagon was having trouble with his rifle—or his nerve. He had yet to fire a shot.

The Colt leaped in his fist when Fargo tagged a second horse, a buckskin with a roached mane. By now the other two mounted men had spotted Fargo's position and opened up on him with a vengeance.

Geysers of sand spat upward as rounds thumped in nineteen to the dozen. Fargo's hat went spinning off his head and a round raked a shallow furrow along the Ovaro's right flank. Still, man and horse stood steady as a granite mountain. The moment Fargo had a decent chance to score a hit at handgun range, he knocked a rider out of his saddle.

The fourth rider, seeing all this and losing his fighting fettle, wheeled his black stallion to flee. Fargo, who looked the other way on many crimes, never gave quarter to murderers. Determined to finish this right, he dropped the stallion with two shots.

"Do it," he shouted when the fourth rider slapped for his short gun, "and I'll drill an air shaft through you!"

That fourth rider, Fargo saw as he walked carefully forward, was an Apache, his long black hair restrained by a rawhide thong. He had the powerful legs and chest typical of his tribe.

"Coyote," Fargo greeted him, recognizing one of the most notorious bandits in the Far West. "Why don't you stay down south in *Apacheria*?"

"Skye Fargo," the Apache responded, still sitting in the sand. "The famous Trailsman, white do-gooder. I was educated by the mission *padres*, remember? I am not welcome in *Apacheria*."

"A murdering scut like you ain't even welcome to his mother. Taking them scalps from your own clan and selling them for bounty in Mexico . . . I always wondered how you sleep at night."

4

"On my back," Coyote responded with his quick, goading grin. "Or on a white man's woman."

Fargo was worried about those other riders catching him off guard. One was still pinned and bawling like a bay steer. The black-suited man in the wagon had the other men covered. But did that damn rifle even work?

"Unbuckle that short iron and toss it toward me," Fargo ordered Coyote. "That knife in your moccasin, too—but slide it, don't throw it."

Fargo moved quickly around, gathering all of the attackers' weapons. The West might be big, but it still contained few people, so he recognized one more face: Joaquin Robles, a road bandit and smuggler from the tiny Mexican village of San Luis. He wore a straw Sonora hat and the white cotton of a Mexican peasant. All four desperadoes wore clothing squirming with beggar lice.

"*El famoso* Fargo," Robles greeted him from gritted teeth, for he was the one pinned under his horse. "You make the big mistake, *verdad*? You did not kill us."

"I'll consider requests," Fargo assured him, aiming the Colt at his head.

"Wait!" The bandit's copper skin paled. "My little joke, eh?"

Fargo whistled when he spotted Robles' rifle in the sand: a fifteen-pound Sharps equipped with a telescopic sight. This wasn't the usual outlaw's gun—somebody was damn eager to assure hits.

The other two prisoners, strangers to Fargo, were both white men. He assumed the names they readily gave him were "summer names." The one calling himself Rick Cully was tall and beanpole thin, with only a slight wound where Fargo's bullet raked his rib cage. Stone Lofley, the fourth man, was silent and brooding, with a broad, blunt, expressionless face that lived up to his first name. Fargo feared him and Coyote most of all.

"A thousand thanks, sir," the young man with the rifle greeted him. He was strong-limbed, his dark hair slicked back with axle grease. "You just saved our lives. My name is Newt Helzer, of Troy Grove, Illinois, and that's my sister Lindy in the wagon."

Fargo nodded curtly, ignoring the hand Newt offered—

with those cunning killers still unsecured, this was no time for parlor manners.

"Name's Skye Fargo," he told the evident greenhorn. "Gather up the ropes off their horses, Newt. We need to get these boys' hands trussed up good before they make a fox play."

"You killed our horses, Fargo, you bastard!" the beanpole calling himself Rick Cully spat out. "The hell we s'posed to do now, *walk*?"

Fargo's strong white teeth flashed through his beard when he grinned. "Congratulations. You guessed it in one."

"Shit! I'm wounded, you heartless son of a bitch! I need doctorin'!"

Fargo, who had once set his own broken arm with a canteen strap, gazed in contempt at the slight wound. How could it have knocked Cully out of the saddle?

"What you *need*," Fargo retorted, "is a set of oysters on you. That bullet barely creased you."

"Like hell! Christ, this wound could mortify."

Fargo nodded. "It might," he agreed cheerfully, "if there's a God."

"All tied up, Mr. Fargo," Newt reported. "All their weapons are loaded in our wagon."

Fargo spoke low in the kid's ear. "Is that rifle of yours even loaded? I didn't see you fire it."

"I tried," Newt said, looking embarrassed. "But nothing happened."

Fargo took the piece and thumbed the hammer to full cock. He pointed at the obviously cracked firing pin. "Hell, this rifle is brand new, yet it ain't worth an old underwear button. You been dry firing it?"

"Dry firing?"

"Snapping the hammer down when the gun's unloaded."

"Oh." Newt flushed. "Hundreds of times. I thought I should practice."

"Practice with a loaded gun. Well, this one's past shooting until it's repaired. Replace it with one we just confiscated."

Both men fell in step to go check on Newt's sister, Fargo leading the Ovaro and sending plenty of cross-shoulder glances toward the captives.

"Essence of lockjaw?" Newt offered Fargo a bottle of Kentucky bourbon.

Fargo cut the dust and wiped his mouth on his sleeve.

"Ain't my way," he told Newt, "to nose a man's back-trail. But just where the hell are you and your sister headed? Right now you're on the trail to Los Angeles. That's not really a destination, just a stepping-off place for men outfitting for the gold mines. And that trade has dwindled lately."

Newt looked like he'd been sucker punched. "Los Angeles? But we're headed farther north for San Francisco. Aren't those the Tehachapi Mountains?" he asked, pointing ahead at some scant-grown hills.

"The Tehachapi range is a couple hundred miles north of here," Fargo replied.

"We're darn lucky we even got this far," Newt admitted. "We fell for John Fremont's lie about the shortcut from Great Salt Lake to California. It's clearly marked on his map."

Fargo shook his head in silent disgust. It was downright sad how few pilgrims spent much time in the map files back home—assuming maps were available, which they often weren't. It was also downright appalling how many pilgrims accepted any map thrust into their hands as reliable.

But Fargo's disgust quickly gave way to sudden pleasure as they drew nearer the wagon and the waiting woman. Despite the heat she wore a black calico skirt, a knitted shawl, the ubiquitous coal-shovel bonnet. She was slender and wasp-waisted with a straining bodice, her wheat blond hair in sausage curls. Big, fetching eyes of liquid green set off a sensuous mouth and startling white teeth.

Newt quickly introduced them.

"Thank you, Mr. Fargo," Malinda "Lindy" Helzer greeted him effusively. "You were so brave. You saved our lives."

"This time," Fargo reminded her. "But despite eight years in the Union, this entire state is still overrun with kill-crazy marauders. And the most dangerous place of all is San Francisco. That's starting to change, but frankly, it's no place for a decent woman, not yet. Any chance you could change your plans?"

Lindy cooled herself with a grass fan, watching Fargo from big, appealing eyes. "Newt and I have already made an initial payment on a boardinghouse. Today's October fifteenth. If we aren't there by the first of November, we lose both the boardinghouse and our money."

"Fifteen days? Lady, that's not likely."

Fargo hooked a thumb over his shoulder toward the four hardcases. These were common frontier thugs who murdered from ambush, not men who mastered the art of draw-shoot killing. However, they had cohorts, plenty of them.

"Just curious," he told Lindy. "Usually these road gangs just rob their victims, shooting over their heads. Nor do they waste a comely female. But look there."

He pointed at the space where a chunk of seat was missing, only inches from Lindy. "Why do I get the distinct impression they were trying to kill you?"

Her eyes fled from his. "How can *I* explain the criminal mind?"

"I wonder . . . anyhow, there's murdering trash like that packed into the hills and mountains. Men of no-church conscience who kill with enjoyment," he warned.

Lindy batted long lashes at Fargo. "Then . . . won't you guide us? We can pay you well."

Temptation sent a little heat squiggle into Fargo's groin—it had been some time since he'd enjoyed the "mazy waltz" with a female.

"Can't," he said reluctantly. "I'm reporting near Los Angeles to ride security for a surveying crew sighting through a railroad to San Francisco."

He glanced into the wagon. "No water?" he said.

"This morning we licked the dew from our gear," Newt admitted. "That's all we've had today."

Fargo looked at both of them and realized they were suffering hard. He also realized they stood damn little chance of reaching San Francisco alive. Of all the decent places in the country to open a boardinghouse, why pick a wide-open hellhole like San Francisco? Fargo was skeptical of the whole story.

"We'll pay you ten dollars a day," Lindy urged, reading Fargo's indecisive face.

"Tell you what," Fargo replied. "That's damn good money. I'll ride with you folks as far as Los Angeles and find you a good man. We'll take these four sage rats with us and turn them over to the law."

A disappointed frown creased Lindy's face. "I'd say we've found a good man in you, Mr. Fargo."

Her eyes took his full measure as she said this. She added a come-hither smile in case he didn't take her meaning. Fargo, feeling that smile in his hip pocket, feared he was on the verge yet again of doing something stupid.

2

Fargo figured enough daylight remained to justify hitting the trail again. Besides, it would be self-torture to make an early stop in this daytime heat. Better to wait—the desert turned blessedly cool at night.

He cautiously freed the trapped rider, Robles. Then, uncoiling the rope from his own saddle horn, Fargo made a lead line and hitched all four prisoners to the tailgate of the wagon.

"Fargo!" shouted the skinny mouthpiece named Rick Cully, who had been listening to the earlier conversation. "You don't *even* want to go to Los Angeles, chum. You'll just be sticking your head in a noose. They don't cotton to law-and-order crusader types like you."

Fargo knew that was true enough. Last time he rode through Los Angeles, there'd been forty-four killings that year without one conviction. The place was catching up to San Francisco as a "heller." Still, he also heard there was now a U.S. marshal and a new jailhouse.

"Tell me something, Cully," Fargo replied. "Since when does a hard twist like you worry about *my* neck? Sounds to me like maybe you're the one doesn't want to go to Los Angeles. 'S'matter . . . your face decorating some wanted posters?"

All four men, surly and uncooperative, stood sweating in the sun behind the wagon. Stone Lofley and Coyote looked especially dangerous to Fargo's experienced eye.

"Hell, just let us go, Fargo," Cully urged. "Be a lot easier."

"When a man tries to put sunlight through me, he ain't

walking away from it. Either I kill him or I jug him. Guess I'm funny that way."

"*Pues,* what about the pretty *mujer*?" Joaquin Robles put in, nodding toward Lindy on the wagon seat. "The shame! You would take such juicy meat among a pack of starving dogs? The big hero, the Trailsman, treating a lady like a whore?"

"Might's well. I treat whores like ladies." Fargo dismissed the cutthroat.

Secretly, however, he was indeed worried about the Mexican's point. This entire state was woman-starved, and Lindy was prime female flesh. It was too late now to avoid Los Angeles—the high-desert country surrounding them canceled out any other route, including turning back. They would be several days getting there, and these four jackals would seize the first opportunity to overpower their captors.

"Know what? I should shoot the no-'count sons of bitches right now," an irritated Fargo remarked to Newt. "They're going to be trouble, you can count on it. You picked out a new rifle? You'll sure's hell need it."

Newt, who had removed his coat and now wore a dusty calfskin vest, reached into the weapons piled in the bed of the wagon. He handed Fargo the fifteen-pound Sharps rifle. Fargo felt Lindy's fluid green eyes taking his measure from the seat up front.

"I like this one," Newt said. "I've already charged it. You approve? It's got a telescopic sight, too. You won't see many of these."

"The piece is excellent," Fargo conceded. "And the seven-hundred grain powder load will stop an express train."

"But then, why the frown?"

"It's a single shot, and at best you'll get off four shots a minute. Keep it for a backup gun and take that Volcanic lever-action instead—shells're only a third of the powder load of the Sharps, but that magazine holds thirty rounds. And it's faster to operate."

"All right," Newt agreed reluctantly. "But I don't need a repeater for courage. I'm ready to die if I must."

"I got a better idea," Fargo barbed when he quit laughing. "Why not be determined to kill your enemy first? In

11

a shooting scrape, especially an ambush, your first shot is often your only shot. That smaller, lighter Volcanic will get you into the fight quicker with lots more firepower."

Fargo opened the Sharps breechblock and pulled the primer cap off the nipple. "Another thing . . . for safety on the trail, keep a percussion rifle loaded but not capped or primed. A hard bump will detonate it."

"Sounds like you know beans from buckshot, Mr. Fargo," Newt gave in, trading the heavy Sharps for the smaller, lever-action Volcanic.

"He certainly does," Lindy chastised her brother while Fargo and Newt set out to collect any water carried on the outlaws' dead mounts. "Are you *sure* we can't convince you to take us to San Francisco, Mr. Fargo? The route so far has been so dangerous. And frankly, what*ever* the gun, Newt couldn't hit a tent from the inside."

"Sorry," Fargo called over his shoulder. "Already gave my word."

Dangerous . . . Fargo bit his tongue. It wasn't the route that was so dangerous, the problem was damn human ignorance. The earliest mountain men to explore the frontier had flourished there. True, some were scalped, but you never heard of one who was sick with anything worse than a hangover or a rotten tooth. With these later pilgrims, however, it was every ailment known to man.

Such as serious and unnecessary eye damage, Fargo thought as he glanced at Newt's red-rimmed, swollen eyes.

"Tell me something," Fargo asked. "I'm just curious."

"About what?"

"Didn't you know, before you left Illinois, that you'd be crossing deserts? Glaring sun, blowing sand and grit, the god-awful reflection off the salt flats and alkali pans?"

Newt nodded, his fresh-scrubbed face eager. "Sure. I read up on all of it. Even memorized names of all the dangerous Indian tribes in the deserts."

"Jesus," Fargo said in disbelief. The kid was worrying about flies while tigers ate him alive. "Then you must have also noticed, whether you left at Saint Joe *or* Independence, how they sell protective goggles practically everywhere?"

Newt looked less brash. Just then another tear oozed from one irritated eye.

"Yeah, now that you mention it," he replied. "For thirty-seven and a half cents a pair. I didn't think about it."

"Obviously. And now you'll be damn lucky if you don't suffer permanent eye damage. Pay attention to things that *matter.*"

"All right," Newt agreed as the two men began pulling canteens. He nodded toward Coyote. "I'll bet that Apache matters plenty. He looks like trouble. He grins every time he looks at you, but he's not amused."

"That Apache is trouble, all right," Fargo agreed. "But all four of those owlhoots are dangerous—dangerous as unstable nitro. Do *not* relax around any of them. These are cold-blooded killers running from the noose. Only, believe me, they don't intend to kill your sister until they've . . . had their use of her."

Newt nodded grimly as they returned to the wagon. "Yeah. I'm green, but not stupid."

"Frankly, Newt, that's debatable," Fargo said bluntly. "Taking a woman like Lindy to *live* in San Francisco? Rape, cholera, flying bullets, constant fires and mud slides . . . a boardinghouse would likely do just as well in Omaha or Kansas City and be a helluva lot safer for a woman."

"She's set on going," Newt said evasively, his eyes fleeing from Fargo's probing gaze.

"Hey, Fargo!" Rick Cully shouted. "I gotta piss like a racehorse! Since you got our hands tied up, how's 'bout sending the skirt back here to aim our nozzles for us?"

All of the men laughed except for the silent, brooding Stone Lofley. Fargo veered over to plant himself in front of Cully.

"Tell you what, beanpole," Fargo offered. "How about we pull it out for you right now and just *leave* it out as a courtesy?"

Fargo hooked a thumb toward the broiling sun, stuck high in the sky as if pegged there. Cully caught his drift, thought about a nasty sunburn down *there,* and lost the smirk.

"That's all right. I can wait," Cully muttered.

"*Pues*, what about *comida*?" Robles chimed in. "*Tenemos hambre.* We are hungry. We have not eaten all day."

Fargo waved a careless hand, shooing this complaint off

like a fly. "Old son, you best fret about Los Angeles and a hemp party. Safe bet you four are on the dodge for serious crimes."

Robles grinned, his knowing eyes meeting those of the other prisoners before he looked at Fargo again.

"Hemp party? *Que broma,* what a joke! It is always amusing," he retorted, "to meet a grown man who believes in fairy tales."

They hadn't rolled twenty feet before Fargo, chafing at the delay, called a halt.

The dry desert air had shrunk the wooden wagon wheels, in turn threatening to pop the iron tires loose. Fargo, hearing them clatter, quickly reinforced them with wooden wedges while the prisoners taunted him.

Again they set off. The afternoon sun, dulled only by the occasional whirling dervish of yellow-brown sand, inched its slow way toward the serrated peaks of the coast range. As if tracking it, the strange little party moved slowly west across the burning Mojave sand, tiny and insignificant in the sterile vastness.

"Not only is there a hell," Newt remarked to his sister, "but looks like we've found it."

"Smartest thing you've said yet," Fargo told him.

Weird and grotesque rock formations, sculpted into strange shapes by eons of wind and sand erosion, rose on their left flank as they passed through Hidden Valley and then Yucca Valley. To their right stretched one of the most barren deserts east of the High Sierra, desert formed when those lofty Sierra peaks arrested the rain clouds.

"Bet you've seen worse deserts, Skye?" Lindy prompted him, her sensuous mouth forming a little moue. She fluttered those long, curving, dark lashes at him. He rode his stallion beside her, keeping a constant eye on the disgruntled line of marching prisoners trudging behind the Dougherty wagon.

"Worse? Let's see . . . the Salt Desert in the Utah Territory is one I'll never cross again. And New Mexico's Jornada del Muerto—"

"Journey of Death," Newt translated for his sister.

"—is just as dry as the Salt. But it's only ninety-three miles across."

"Really? Well, all this sand," Lindy complained, "is lodging in my throat, nose, and eyes."

Your lovely throat, perfect nose, bewitching eyes, Fargo amended. He smiled politely, but secretly he was increasingly worried about his Ovaro. Long days spent crossing hard-baked ground had left the stallion sore-footed. Without relief soon, the stalwart pinto would draw up lame, and then Fargo would be in a world of hurt no pretty girl could fix with her charms.

"I've noticed," he remarked to Lindy, "that your wagon is packed mighty light for two people planning to settle in San Francisco."

"Our new boardinghouse is furnished," Newt spoke up.

"Taxes are high up there," Fargo persisted. "And, on average, the business district burns to the ground once a year. What happens if you lose everything? There's no county poorhouses out here."

"Soon as we get there," Newt replied, "I'm planning to start a fallback business selling firewood to steamboats up on the Columbia."

"Sounds like a levelheaded plan," Fargo said, still not believing them.

By now the late afternoon sun was balanced above the nearby San Bernardino Mountains. Several times, without warning, tornadic winds had sprung up in an eyeblink, the billows of yellow-brown dust destroying all sense of direction. At such times Fargo drew nearer the cursing prisoners, Colt to hand.

"Moses on the mountain!" Lindy exclaimed bitterly after one of these sudden sandstorms had abated. She brushed the sand from her black calico dress, those seductive eyes watching Fargo. "I know, Skye . . . I look like a widow, right? Out west a girl *always* has to look like a widow because only dark clothing doesn't show the dirt."

"Just pull that dress right off, sweet britches!" Rick Cully goaded from the back. "I'll keep the sun off the front of you!"

"Stow it, mouthpiece," Fargo warned him, "or I'll gag you and take your boots."

"Huzzah!" Newt sang out. "Signs of life up ahead."

Newt meant the Mormon farming commune of San Bernardino, tucked into the mountain pass between the high

desert and the California coast. Even this late in the year
the hills surrounding the well-irrigated fields were teemin
with sweet clover, some slopes golden-yellow with arrow
root blossoms. As they drew nearer they spotted men i
the fields wearing the characteristic wreath beard of th
Mormons.

"Shouldn't we stop for water?" Newt asked. "Ther
looks to be plenty of dry ground still ahead."

Fargo glanced back at the prisoners, their faces brass
and hostile in the waning sunlight. Coyote's black-butto
eyes mocked him with the promise of a hard death; Ston
Lofley's granite-slab face could have been the entrance t
an unmarked tomb.

"Better not stop," he replied to Newt. "The locals ar
law-abiding and won't welcome this crew. Besides, Mor
mons don't like it when outsiders camp in the valley, an
if we stop now we'll never get beyond it before dark."

"But the horses need water—"

"Actually," Fargo cut him off, "there's usually water i
any desert. The trick is to know where and how to ex
tract it."

"A trick Skye surely knows," Lindy said smugly, watch
ing Fargo. "He knows *lots* of useful tricks, I'll bet."

"Speaking of water, Fargo," Cully's grating voice spok
up, "we're spittin' cotton back here, man! How's 'bout
sup?"

"Not until we make camp and the sun sets," Fargo re
plied. "Otherwise it'll just turn into sweat."

"Yeah, know-it-all? Well, why'n'cha just lick the *swea*
off my bal—Jesus!"

Fargo had his belly full of this mouthy bastard and hi
filthy talk. Before Cully could finish his taunt, Fargo ha
pulled the imposing Arkansas toothpick from its boo
sheath.

"There's a lady up there," Fargo said, steady eyes back
ing up his no-nonsense tone. "You can take this to th
bank—you keep up the barracks talk, and I'll slice you
tongue out."

"Put that pigsticker away, no need to have a conniptio
fit," Cully muttered before he wisely fell silent.

Fargo was damn glad he would soon be on the mountai
trails again, shed of this bunch and earning badly neede

wages. It was the same sad story—Fargo, like the mountain men before him, ran from the relentless pressure of civilization. Ironically, in his flight he helped create the paths and trails used to overtake him.

Then there were these four criminal misfits. Despite his long experience at locking horns with outlaw types, Fargo felt especially intimidated by this hard-bitten crew. As for Newt, he was a nice enough fellow, but so green he'd not likely survive San Francisco *if* he ever got there. And Lindy? Robles was right, meat to starving curs.

"Penny for your thoughts," Lindy's voice jolted him.

"Just wondering why you never glance back at the prisoners," Fargo lied, keeping his voice low so they wouldn't hear. "Most women are morbidly curious to peek at outlaws. Somebody you're afraid you might recognize?"

Those shimmering green eyes could not withstand Fargo's scrutiny.

"My stars!" she protested a bit too emphatically. "Am I to flirt with mudsill ruffians when a man like you is close enough to . . . touch?"

"Good answer," Fargo agreed with a smile, admiring the well-turned ankle she took pains to let him see. Slim and white, the skin smooth as lotion. This little filly, he told himself, was looking to be mounted.

"Sun's going low," Newt remarked. "Shall we camp in that little meadow just ahead? There's some grass for our horses."

Fargo was slow to reply. For some time now he had been spotting, from the corner of his left eye, dust puffs rising above the southern horizon, approaching from the direction of Arizona or even Mexico.

Coyote had seen them, too, and smiled now at Fargo, nodding as if to say: *The worm has turned, hair-face.*

"Camp here, Mr. Fargo?" Newt repeated a bit louder.

Fargo refocused and glanced quickly around. He shook his head.

"It's wide open. When you pick a campsite," he advised Newt, an attentive lad eager to learn, "look for water, concealment, shelter from the wind, and a good view to your backtrail. Let's go on a little farther."

Again Fargo glanced at the ghostlike dust puffs, then caught Coyote grinning at him.

"Coyote," Fargo murmured to himself, suddenly remembering. *Shunk* manitu . . . "the Coyote." The name, given to an Indian, was never accidental. It was reserved for the best liar and trickster in any tribe.

Fargo dropped back until he was beside the Apache.

"Something you'd like to say?" Fargo invited, looking down from the saddle.

Coyote pointed his chin toward the dust puffs. "Comanches. They have killed more whites than any other tribe, Fargo," the Apache responded softly. "And now they are coming for you."

3

San Francisco

"No damn way, Jack, am I ever going to truckle to people of rank. Already the first voices of 'reform' in the *Californian* and other newspapers claim I'm establishing Tammany politics out west. And so I am, for Boss Tweed's political machine is unstoppable. *Let* the crapsheets whine like spineless bitches. The final decision will be left to Judge Moneybags, a good friend indeed."

Prescott Wagner fell silent and turned away from the wet windowpane to face his seated subordinate.

"The crapsheets also whine about the 'divisive factionalism' of American society, Jack, but I say it's good for business. Free-Soilers versus slavers, expansionists versus nonexpansionists, Indian lovers versus the extermination crowd—hell, even Catholics and Protestants are at daggers drawn. The jingo press fans the fires even hotter. And meantime?"

His bored listener and most useful lackey, "Terrible Jack" Slade, finally realized he was supposed to respond during this pause. "Yeah, meantime?"

"Meantime, the high-and-mighty in Congress are getting drunk, *in session* mind you, and beating each other senseless with canes. The whole damn country is grazing loco weed, and I say let 'er rip! It's made me so rich I can't count all of it. A 'unified' nation would hang me."

Wagner was short but powerfully built, still vigorous though his flashy muttonchops showed threads of silver. Charismatic and hot-tempered, he was a take-charge man, part of America's new master class: politicians who had perfected the Great Commoner act, pandering to the masses while turning vile crimes into "acts of patriotism."

Something occurred to him, and a frown turned his features mean.

"But despite my mountain of money, Jack," he remarked, "I'm not going to ride out this imminent scandal. Not with a pregnant woman of good family involved. So what can't be survived *must* be prevented."

Wagner owned, among other notable properties, the first icehouse built in the city. He had even ordered his own mint bed planted, and was now sipping a delicious julep.

"Prevented," he repeated with heavy emphasis. "I have it, from a reliable source, that the new prosecutor has worked out some arrangement with the Helzer woman. She's on her way here now. If she testifies, it all comes out. And you know the old saying: the shit rolls downhill. After they leave me dancing on air, you'll be next."

"It's the knot, for sure," agreed Slade. "But all this speechifying of yours makes it hard to take your point, boss. Are you saying what I *think* you're saying?"

Instead of answering right away, Wagner strolled across the plank floor of his offices on Sacramento Street, gazing out the window into the damp, foggy night. The rain, a drizzle now, had fallen all day long with a steady sizzling noise, once again turning the city's clay streets into dangerous, liquid-mud quagmires. This street also served as the city dump, and the submerged garbage often tripped horses. One rider had drowned in several feet of mud thick as gumbo. Wagner had even seen an entire horse and wagon swallowed up.

This was the way he liked the city, and the way he planned to keep it—dangerous, devoid of law, and best of all, *profitable*. Unfortunately for his plans, however, recent migrants to San Francisco included even the Brahmin population of New England. That meant decency, laws, "public outrage."

"What I'm saying," he finally replied, turning around to study his subordinate from cold black eyes that pierced like bullets, "is inescapable. I always figure percentages and angles, Jack, before I render a decision—you know that by now. It appears that our . . . four-man expeditionary force has bollixed up their mission down south. You may have to finish the job, and there's not much time left."

Slade mulled all that for a minute. His angular face, covered with reddish beard stubble tough as bore bristles, seldom revealed his feelings—not that Wagner believed he ever had any. Terrible Jack Slade was the most notorious ruffian and bullyboy in the state, leader of the *aguardiente*, the saloon set in northern California.

The ruthless vigilante leader always carried the special blacksnake whip that was now curled around his left forearm—known widely as "Judge Lash." Sharp pieces of flint and obsidian, embedded in the popper, could shred a man's skin to bloody ribbons.

"Cully—now I can see him mucking it up," Slade finally replied. "Rick can't stop running his mouth, and on a job talkers just cause trouble. But Stone? Now that boy is a steady hand, and so are the Mexer and the 'pache they hired down there to side them. I know 'em both."

"I'll take your word for it, but something definitely went wrong. I've got a man planted down south in the Mormon settlement. He used a pocket relay to splice into the telegraph line at San Bernardino. Sent me a message that all four men are now prisoners."

"Prisoners?" Slade's face remained blank, but disbelief seeped into his tone. "*That* bunch? Prisoners of who? Satan and his hellhounds?"

Wagner had guessed the "who" by now, but he was in no hurry to tell his toady. Again he turned to the streaked windowpane, suddenly worried anew. He had been on hand, barely a decade earlier, when this city began as a mud-cove flat called Yerba Buena. Someone also called it "the ugly duckling" of the Far West, and that it certainly was.

Wagner, through secret alliances with the worst of the criminal element, used murder and terror to steal gold claims from foreigners prospecting the nearby hills. He had already made his first million by the time the first solid brick buildings had begun to replace mud huts and driftwood hovels. Why *should* he have any less than those living in their turreted mansions back east?

"Who took them captive?" Wagner finally replied. "That's not certain. But it's a tall, bearded man in buckskins, riding a black-and-white pinto stallion."

Even now Slade's poker face impressed Wagner. But a muscle in his cheek jumped. "Skye goddamn Fargo, huh? Yeah, that explains it."

Wagner bristled at the note of surrender he detected in Slade's voice, as if suddenly God Almighty had descended into California and harps would now replace guns. Wagner feared no "Western heroes." He had learned the art of easy-go killing as a dragoon in the Mexican War. After the war he led a gang that preyed on forty-niners in the Sierra, murdering scores of them and amassing a fortune. That money, wisely invested in Yerba Buena, now had him poised to become mayor of San Francisco, then governor of California.

Unless, that is, those four captured men were forced to stand trial. Wagner knew he would be exposed, ruined, hanged. But it was Malinda Helzer's testimony, more than any, that would sink him. When the facts came out about her sister, he'd be torn apart by a howling male mob before he ever reached the gallows.

"So what if it is Fargo?" Wagner demanded. "You may never have to deal with the problem. I've got two men down in Los Angeles, too, and that's where he's headed."

"Never said I was afraid of the job," Slade retorted. "Men like Fargo get talked up big, but they don't buffalo me. Besides, the jasper who plants Fargo can get rich displaying his head in a jar. And old Judge Lash here would cotton to a chance at peeling that bastard's hide like a wet label."

Slade touched his cruelly modified whip, evoking an approving smile from his employer.

"*That's* the spirit, Jack. Sin bravely! By now you have surely noticed that I am a man of large-scale ambitions. Soon I will no longer be a businessman, just a pure speculator—all I will make is money. As my tide rises, your boat will be lifted too."

"Un-hunh," Slade said, bored with Wagner's damn wordy speeches. "All right, so Fargo has to be killed. What about Rick and them—plug 'em?"

"If you can manage to spring them, do it. Men like that

are useful to have around. If not, kill them or they might end up on a witness stand. But we *must* kill the girl, and whoever's bringing her, before the November first trial or we're goners.''

For some time now shots, one or two in each burst, had been exploding throughout the raucous city. Both men ignored them each time, recognizing the familiar and harmless pattern of celebration shots.

Suddenly, however, there were three shots, and the men locked gazes. One or two shots usually meant harmless celebration; three were more ominous.

"Killing," Slade said in a bored tone, reaching for his flap hat. "I better get down there."

"Find out who did it," Wagner said. "If it's a white man, see what he'll pay if we hang a Chinaman for it. Be discreet. If it's a Mexer, have your boys lynch him immediately in the interest of law and order."

Slade nodded. "Need me back here tonight?"

"Yes. We need to make plans for your possible ride south. If my men in Los Angeles bungle the job, it'll be your show. It's two weeks until that court date. Stay on Fargo and the girl like heat rash until you've killed them both."

Fargo had rejected Newt's choice of campsite in favor of an edge-of-desert oasis only thirty minutes beyond it. A stream originating in the San Bernardino Mountains splashed over smooth boulders, a line of juniper trees formed both a screen and a windbreak.

"Tomorrow we'll enter the mountain pass," Fargo explained to Newt and his sister. "It's a long pass, narrow and twisting, but all downhill along a pretty good trail. We'll emerge down on the plain, but we'll still have at least another full day before we reach Los Angeles."

"Or," Newt suggested in a wheedling tone, "the three of us could tie these smelly cutthroats to a tree and turn north now toward San Francisco. There's a road, the Los Padres Trail, on my map. We'll pay ten dollars a day, Skye, if you'll take us."

Fargo's eyes shifted to the "smelly cutthroats," each tied to his own tree well away from his companions.

"Sorry," he replied. "We part company in Los Angeles.

But let me warn you, forget the Los Padres Trail or *any* interior route to San Francisco."

"But why? The big gold rush of forty-nine is petering out now after almost a decade," Newt protested. "I read how the criminals have moved elsewhere."

"Then you read hogwash. Sure, most of the gold is played out, but there's still dangerous towns and camps scattered throughout the mountains. No law but their own. Take the coast, it's easier and more settled."

"But exactly what is the danger?" Lindy pressed, her loose-hanging hair gleaming like spun gold in the firelight. "More road gangs like this one?"

That and Indian "gangs," Fargo thought when a nearby coyote—he hoped—raised its long howl that ended in a series of yipping barks. Those dust puffs had remained visible until sunset, moving steadily closer. Fargo wasn't fooled by the apparent long distance. These braves were most likely making good time on their special running horses, kept just for the chase or war parties.

"One reason to stay along the coast," Fargo replied bluntly, "is you yourself, pretty lady. Most men on the frontier aren't exactly the type familiar with opera houses and good grooming, especially the prospecting crowd in the interior. Out here, a beauty like you stands out like a brass spittoon in an undertaker's parlor."

"Another reason, I'll bet, is vigilante fever, right?" Newt tossed in. "It's all over the newspapers back home. And even back there armed mobs are controlling rough places like Sedalia, Missouri, and Baxter Springs in the Kansas Territory."

The kid was green, but not stupid. Fargo had borne close witness to the rise of vigilantism in the decade of the 1850s. Back east, the new "manufactories" were taking trade from thousands of skilled workers, unleashing on the West hordes of angry, desperate men who were turning to lawlessness. Then, in 1851, Brigham Young deported a large group of his banished criminals to California, where the situation was already chaotic. Soon thugs and ex-cons controlled the government, and the "police forces" were flush with criminals.

Fargo watched the Ovaro, grazing nearby, lift his nose toward the south, sampling the air. Then he started cropping grass again. Fargo would keep a close eye on the stallion, who was trained to give warning at the Indian smell.

"Vigilantes, huh?" Fargo finally repeated thoughtfully as he gnawed on a strip of jerked buffalo. "Glad you said that word, Newt—you just jogged my memory."

He nodded toward the tied-up prisoners at the very edge of the firelight. "That one who hasn't opened his mouth to say a word? I could swear I saw him a few years ago up in San Francisco, only it was still called Yerba Buena then. He was a leader of the Hounds."

"The who?" Lindy asked.

"They were the 'vigilante' bunch that terrorized the city back then. Still do, though not so openly. Outright criminals wrapping themselves in the flag. Didn't take long for their brand of justice to infect the nearby gold fields. 'Trials' last about five minutes. Foreigners and peaceful Indians take the brunt of it. I know of one entire California tribe that was wiped out because one Indian boy was accused of stealing a blanket from a tent."

Fargo trailed off, watched the four men again for a minute, then looked at Lindy. "But I'm thinking these four, if any of 'em are Hounds, are mighty far from their nest— why? With all the easy pickings up their way, why drift down to the empty desert country?"

"*I* certainly can't tell you," Lindy replied, suddenly busy at her long hair with a horn comb.

Can't or won't, Fargo thought.

"Hey, Fargo!" Coyote's gravel-pan voice brayed from the darkness. "Hear that 'coyote' a few minutes ago? Gonna sleep good tonight, white man?"

"What's he mean?" Lindy demanded, her voice tight with nervousness.

"We may have Indians nosing our backtrail," Fargo said calmly. Lindy gasped and Newt dropped his tin coffee cup.

"Indians?" Newt repeated. "Criminy! Hostile?"

"They ain't likely mission-school Indians," Fargo conceded. "Since they're coming up from Mexico, prob'ly Comanches or Apaches taking the long way back from a raid."

Some newspapers back east boasted that the "red aborigines" had been pacified in California. But the wise waved it aside, and so did Fargo. True, local tribes such as the

25

Mojaves and Modocs were not casual killers, and West Coast Indians were less warlike, in general. But this part of lower California was often raided, with pitiless brutality, by Plains tribes.

Newt swallowed audibly. "Comanches or Apaches— which would be worse?"

Both tribes were double rough, but Fargo didn't even have to debate the choice. Unlike many, he had never considered Indians depraved or evil. But without question the Comanches were capable of an instant brutality that was shocking.

"Comanches," he replied. "Apaches are killers, but not big on torture. Comanches have killed and tortured more whites than any other tribe."

"Are they close by?" Newt asked, nervously studying the inky fathoms of darkness surrounding them.

"Could be. But not right on us yet, according to my horse. Unfortunately, Comanches will attack at night. So will Apaches, for that matter. Don't be wandering far."

"Darn it," Lindy fussed. "There goes my cool bath in the mountain stream."

Fargo's lips eased apart in a grin. "Why? As long as you have an armed guard along."

"Who wants to see his own sister naked?" Newt joked. "Looks like the awful task is yours, Skye."

"I'm one to volunteer," Fargo joked back. "But it's really up to Lindy."

By way of reply she stood up immediately, smoothed her skirt, then grabbed Fargo's rein-callused hand and tugged him to his feet.

The desert chilled considerably after dark, but tonight a balmy chinook was blowing up from the Pacific coast of Mexico. Fargo had tossed his box of faulty ammo and loaded the Henry with shells seized from the prisoners. He carried his rifle in his left hand, his right resting on the small of Lindy's back.

"No corset," he said approvingly as they walked toward the stream.

"Makes it quicker to strip naked," she said teasingly, and Fargo's sudden arousal forced him to adjust his step. She noticed and laughed.

26

"Got family back in Troy Grove?" he asked.

"I . . . had a twin sister," Lindy replied. "She died."

Fargo waited, but when she added no more he left it alone.

"And you," she said, perhaps to stop his questioning. "So you're going to be working on a railroad between Los Angeles and San Francisco? It's hard to envision a man like you swinging a pickax."

Fargo laughed. He had little hope for this new railroad project. Baking summertime heat would warp the rails out of alignment just as he'd seen it happen in Mexico.

"Sure's hell is hard to envision me doing pick-and-shovel work," he replied. "Darlin', I don't accept any job that pulls me outta the saddle. I'll just be riding guard for the workers."

They crested a sandy rise tufted with bunch grass. A luminous full moon showed a grassy slope below them, leading down to the chuckling stream. The San Bernardino Mountains cut rounded black silhouettes in the western sky.

"Ask you something?" Fargo said. "The wind's been kicking up something fierce, but that light dress you've got on hangs straight as a door. You a magician?"

"Yes, and I'll reveal my female trick. Reach down and grab my hem."

Fargo's breathing was already quickening, but his survival instincts kept him careful. He sent a cross-shoulder glance toward the Ovaro, who was still grazing quietly. Fargo also placed three fingertips against the ground to check for vibrations. When he detected nothing, he lay his Henry in the grass and knelt before Lindy like a man proposing.

"Lead weights sewed into the hem," he said with a grin, feeling the tiny weights.

"How 'bout my . . . limbs?" Lindy suggested, her voice going a little husky. "Long as you're down there, might as well inspect them, too."

Even hot-blooded Lindy couldn't bring herself to say "legs." In Fargo's day men were not breast starved—fashion encouraged women to reveal nearly all of their breasts. However, female legs were puritanically covered from ankles to hips. Men rarely saw—much less touched—a bare leg and, thus, lusted constantly for this forbidden fruit. Lindy's invitation now sent blood roaring into Fargo's ears.

His hands glided up her bare legs, feeling skin smooth and flawless as polished ivory. Over those slim, well-turned ankles his hands moved, then along supple, trim calves, and higher still until he caressed her chamois-soft inner thighs. By now Lindy was trembling to his touch and Fargo's breathing was ragged.

"You definitely pass inspection," he assured her.

"I *should* bathe now," Lindy said in a breathless voice. "But . . . as long as you're down there inspecting so nicely, you don't *have* to stop now. Go higher, please?"

Happy to oblige, Fargo slid one hand up her creamy thigh until his fingers encountered furry, moist heat. A keening noise escaped Lindy when his talented fingers began to cosset her love nest, going faster and faster until her pearl nubbin was swollen hard. Her liquid arousal was actually beading on his wrist.

"Damn, girl," Fargo marveled, "you *are* ready and so'm I. Peel that dress off and let's take care of this."

"Yes, *sir*," she said eagerly, naked even before Fargo got the flap of his buckskins untied. Fargo marveled at the naked beauty in the clear but flattering moonlight. The blond hair fell loose over her slim white shoulders, and her impressive breasts were capped by huge, strawberry nipples. The hips were wide and flaring, the stomach smooth and flat.

"You'll do to take along," Fargo assured her.

"It's time to inspect *you*," she said playfully, slapping his hands away from his trousers to finish the job herself. A moment later: "My stars!" she exclaimed as she fumbled his full length out into view. "Is that gorgeous thing even legal? Well, I've heard *every*thing is bigger in the West. Guess it's true—but what are we waiting for?"

Tugging Fargo down with her into the cool grass, Lindy surprised him by cocking one leg to straddle him. Very few women, in his vast experience, dared to try anything but the missionary.

"Hope you don't mind?" she whispered as she bent his shaft to the perfect entry angle. "See, it's lots better for me up here. Rubs my . . . little button better. Just relax and let me pleasure us both."

Fargo felt the swollen tip of his manhood parting her nether lips. Then he gasped when she plunged down his full, curving length, sending pleasure surges through his entire body. He steadied her with one hand on each of her taut butt cheeks. This position also had the advantage of hanging those luscious globes of hers right over his face.

"Oh, Skye! Skye Fargo, you wicked, *wicked* man! Oh, that is so good, sooo . . . *OH*!"

Lindy, already firing off pent-up climaxes, began plunging up and down harder, more rapidly, while Fargo took her pliant nipples into his mouth and teased her even more. Neither one of them could hold off long under this total sensual assault.

Lindy, writhing wildly as she milked Fargo with her love muscle, cried out when the biggest climax yet surprised her. Fargo, unable to hold off longer, lifted her completely off the ground when he spent himself deep inside her.

The two exhausted lovers lay in a postorgasmic daze for uncounted minutes, aware only of the splashing stream and their cooling bodies.

"Just think, Skye," her voice finally said close to his ear. "Besides ten dollars a day, if you guide us to San Francisco we'll also have this. I'd like more—lots more, wouldn't you?"

Fargo rolled up on one elbow to reply. Suddenly the Ovaro loosed his trouble whicker. From camp, Newt cursed loudly. A moment later a gunshot shattered the desert quiet, and once again Skye Fargo was fumbling to close his pants at the wrong damn moment.

4

As he raced down the sandy slope, Fargo expected to hear the shrill Comanche kill-cry at any moment. He cursed himself for underestimating the proximity of the earlier dust puffs. If Comanches had already begun to attack the camp, it was too late now for any effective defense.

Instead, he encountered an unexpected spectacle. Joaquin Robles had somehow gotten free and was now locked in a wild dustup with Newt. The Mexican's straw hat lay broken on the ground, and his white cotton clothes were filthy and torn. A two-shot derringer also lay near the grappling men, one hammer down.

"I'll be damned," Fargo remarked to Lindy. "Your bookish brother is doing the hurt dance on that killer."

"Newt may be a greenhorn," Lindy said proudly, "but he's a lumberjack by trade and very strong."

Obviously, Fargo realized as he watched the kid subdue Robles—a big, burly man himself—with a few head-slams to the ground. Moments later the brain-stunned bandit quit struggling and began singing "La Paloma Blanca." When he'd returned to his senses and was securely tied up again, Fargo asked Newt what the hell happened.

"I'm not sure," the panting youth admitted. "I dozed off after tethering the team horses in new grass. Your pinto's loud snorts woke me. I spotted the Mexican trying to lure your horse without much success. When I charged at him, he fired that"—Newt pointed to the derringer lying nearby—"at me almost point blank. But your stallion bumped his arm at the moment he fired. Skye, it sounds crazy, but I think that horse deliberately saved my life."

30

"Wouldn't be the first time he's done that. If he did," Fargo said, feeling chagrined, "he was only making up for my mistakes. I missed that hideout gun when I took Robles' weapons. See the little foldout knife under the barrel?" he added, picking up the weapon. "Must be how he cut his ropes."

Fargo walked from tree to tree, checking the other three prisoners' ropes and then searching them good for hideout weapons.

"Hey, Fargo," Rick Cully greeted him, "I'm warning you for your own good: Let us go now. Your 'reputation' won't be worth a whorehouse token in Los Angeles."

"It's your reputation you better worry about, not mine."

"Still got grass on your clothes, I see, from gettin' your ashes hauled. Boy, you had that hot little piece howling like a timber wolf. Bring her over here, why'n'cha? I ain't too proud for sloppy seconds."

"Yessir, a joker in every deck," Fargo said, barely restraining himself from violence—garbage or not, Cully couldn't hit back. Fargo moved on to Stone Lofley and Coyote. Lofley, as usual, remained silent and brooding, his face expressionless yet explosively dangerous. Coyote, however, began shaking with mirth the moment Fargo arrived.

"Joaquin had to try his escape, Trailsman," the Apache greeted him. "The Comanches are coming, and that tribe hates Mexicans with a blood vengeance. Almost as much as they hate white Tejanos. I like you, Fargo. Saddle your stallion right now, and perhaps you can still save yourself. The girl and her brother are doomed. Leave, Fargo, or face three days of screaming torture before you die."

In fact Coyote wasn't being melodramatic—those Comanches probably were coming, with blood in their eyes. Fargo had been yondering out west for most of his life. He had witnessed or suffered shootings, stabbings, kidnappings, attacks on mail riders and freighters, ambushes by Indians, bear attacks, deliberate train wrecks, various scrapes running into the many hundreds. Life out west was vastly more dangerous, and therefore men simply had to be willing to face the risks. These Comanches were just one more turn in the trail of his life.

"Coyote, you seem pretty sure these Comanches will call you brother when they catch up to us," Fargo said as he stood back up. "But there's no love lost between your tribe and theirs. Besides . . . I have a Comanche scalp in my saddlebag. What if it's dangling from *your* sash when those braves swoop down on us?"

Fargo had no such scalp and knew only a fool would carry one. He grinned when Coyote's eyes suddenly widened in fright.

"Touch of Old Tanglefoot?" Newt asked, proffering the bottle of bourbon when Fargo returned to the fire.

Fargo accepted the bottle, took a sweeping-deep slug, then sat down on a flat rock. Lindy was busy brushing out her hair. She smiled coyly at Fargo, her startling white teeth gleaming in the firelight.

"Now, what's all this talk about Comanches?" Newt demanded. "You mentioned them earlier, too. Are they really going to attack us?"

"That's not certain. An Indian is a notional creature. But if it comes to that," Fargo assured him, "won't be much of an 'attack.' There's two of us versus a band of, prob'ly, anywhere from forty to a hundred braves. And a Comanche on horseback is the best killing machine in the West. Two of us fighting them would be like trying to hold back the ocean with a broom."

Lindy stopped brushing, watching Fargo. "But . . . then what *will* we do?"

"Whatever it takes. When it comes to survival, fighting is only one option—usually not the best. Running is out of the question, for us, but there's always deception."

"Deception?" Lindy repeated. "How so?"

Fargo shook his head. "Can't say until I do it. I usually work up a trick on the fly—it's the enemy who determines your strategy."

"Deception," Newt repeated, liking the concept. "Boy oh boy, does *that* make sense, Skye. I read in *Leslie's Weekly* that the U.S. Army is spending almost one million dollars for every Indian killed. At that rate the country will go broke without defeating one major tribe."

"Straight words. Matter fact, America oughta be handling this entire Indian problem the smart way, not the hard way."

"Hard to imagine smarts defeating savages," Lindy admitted.

"Be worth a try," Fargo insisted. "By nature an Indian

is superstitious and loves magic and spectacle, right? Well, all we had to do was send in a few advance regiments of jugglers and magicians. But no, we put John on the scrap and now he's taking our hair."

Fargo's gaze cut to Lindy. All this chitchat was interesting enough, but a question still nagged at him: why did he have the strong impression that Lindy could not even glance at the captives? Of course a decent woman would keep her distance from such trail trash. Still, simple curiosity should impel at least an occasional glance at them. Fargo played a vague hunch.

"Lindy?"

"Mmm?"

"Which one of those four prisoners," Fargo asked calmly, "have you seen somewhere before? Or is it more than one of them?"

The hand working her brush stopped for a few seconds, then resumed.

"Oh, Skye, you harbor some silly notions," she dismissed him. "How would I know any of them? I've just arrived out here."

"Whatever you say," Fargo replied, dropping it even though he still didn't believe her. "Are you carrying a weapon?"

"No, of course not."

"Well, you should be," Fargo insisted, handing her the derringer Robles had coughed up. "Especially the way your brother shoots. Keep this on your person at all times."

He turned to Newt. "You and me'll split the guard tonight. We've all got a rough job ahead—if we get down on to the coastal plain, Comanches won't likely follow us. There's cannons and howitzers all over down there, and Indians fear the big-talking guns."

"In other words," Newt said, "it's going to be a race to the coast? With us going at a walking pace to accommodate the prisoners?"

Fargo nodded. " 'Fraid so. That two-horse team of yours is worn out. Four more people in your wagon would kill them in this heat and sand. And my stallion is on the verge of a limp from sore feet. I'll have to lead him."

Newt lowered his voice. "Why not just shoot the prisoners if it's them or us?"

"If I was ever tempted," Fargo confessed. "And it may come to that. But only as a last resort."

"Skye's not a murderer, Newt," Lindy put in. "If some-body out here doesn't stand for law and order, it will never be established."

Her tone had turned suddenly passionate, and Fargo suspected she was talking about something specific, not just waxing eloquent. Noting his curiosity, she avoided his probing gaze.

"I guess you're right, sis," Newt agreed. "We must pass through the bitter waters before we reach the sweet, huh?"

"I'll give you a cast-iron guarantee the bitter waters are coming," Fargo agreed. "I'm not so sure about the sweet."

During the rest of the night Fargo and Newt switched off on guard duty every two hours. Worried about those advancing Comanches, Fargo roused Newt and Lindy well before sunrise.

"Hey, Fargo!" Coyote's still sleepy but goading voice called out from the grainy darkness. "You know them Comanches will gang-rape your woman before they stone her into silence. And they'll make *you* watch all of it."

"Keep flapping your gums, shit heel," Fargo called back, reminding him of an earlier threat, "and there'll be a Comanche scalp tied to your sash."

"Maybe so better not," Coyote replied, deliberately breaking into "Indian English" to taunt Fargo. However, he wisely shut up.

"He's right, though, isn't he?" Lindy asked Fargo quietly as she rustled up a batch of ash pone for breakfast. "That's how it would be?"

The Trailsman nodded. "Sure. But I got no plans to let you fall into their hands."

She smiled, forming balls of moist cornmeal and tossing them right into the hot ashes to bake.

"After watching you capture four tough men by yourself yesterday, Skye, I trust you. But honestly . . . why would an obviously intelligent man like you choose to live out west? It seems terribly dangerous."

"But you're coming out here to live, aren't you?" Fargo reminded her.

She looked momentarily flustered. "Yes, of course. I . . .

34

I mean, out in the open, dangerous parts that you seem to prefer."

"It's plenty dangerous, all right. But I've been back east, too, and I'll take my chances out here."

"Then . . . if you like it so much, why don't you want me and Newt living in San Francisco?"

"Because I'm Western born and bred and know the ways out here. And because some say San Francisco is the most violent hellhole in the country. You and Newt both seem like fine people, but you're way too green to face the dangers."

Fargo left it at that—dawn was now a rose flush on the horizon and the team still needed to be hitched. While Lindy and Newt finished breaking camp, Fargo climbed the nearest rock tumble to gain a view toward the south.

"Shit-oh-dear," he whispered when he saw the boiling columns of dust.

The Comanches, realizing where their quarry must be headed, were no longer holding back their horses. They intended to strike before Fargo's group could clear the long, winding pass through the San Bernardino Mountains.

About three hours out at that rate, Fargo estimated as he started back toward camp. And in three hours, his slow group would barely be into the pass.

Of course, they'd stop at this camp first to read sign, Fargo reminded himself. Why waste any opportunity to begin the only strategy that might possibly save himself and the others: deception.

By now the sun was up, already heating the dry air. Fargo was halfway back to camp when he remembered that no Indians would raid into enemy ranges without sending out a scout. This time he kept his skyline even lower as he ascended the rock tumble again, eyes searching much closer.

There . . . Fargo spotted a blur of movement about a hundred yards out—a Comanche brave in buckskins and knee-length moccasins, sneaking forward across sand almost the same color as his clothing. A claybank pony was tethered in a swale behind him. Fargo guessed the short rifle in his hand was a stolen Mexican Army carbine.

Fargo rarely struck without giving a man a fighting chance. He levered a round into the Henry's chamber, hoping these bullets were sound. Then he stood up atop the highest rock, fully exposed to the Comanche below.

The brave froze in place for a full minute, deciding what to do.

"Your call, John," Fargo said in a patient whisper. "Stick or quit."

The Comanche decided to stick. In seconds the carbine was braced in his shoulder socket and he was peppering Fargo's position with lead.

Bullets whanged off the rocks all around him as Fargo, taking more time than the reckless Comanche, sought his bead. Most men worried about getting off the first shot quick in a sudden showdown. Fargo had learned long ago that the most important thing was to stay calm, aim carefully and fire only when you had a sure bead.

So he refused to flinch or lose focus as bullets hornet-buzzed past his ears, tugged at his clothing, and ricocheted between his legs. When Fargo had his front sight center of mass on the brave's chest, he squeezed off one round. A scarlet blossom plumed from the Comanche's chest and he folded to the ground, mortally wounded but still twitching. Taking no pleasure in it, Fargo aimed carefully and put a quick finishing shot in his head—far more humane than leaving a seriously wounded man out here to suffer.

"My God, Skye!" a pallid Lindy greeted him back at the campsite. "What was all that shooting?"

"Ran into a Comanche," Fargo explained as he picked up his saddle and lugged it toward the Ovaro.

"Did you . . . I mean . . . where is he?"

"Gone to hunt the white buffalo," Fargo replied cryptically.

"That means Skye killed him," Newt explained when Lindy frowned, not understanding.

"Just one?" she persisted.

"Yeah, but legions of red sons are right behind him."

Lindy pestered him with more questions, but Fargo ignored her for the critical job of inspecting his tack. He checked his saddle and pad for burrs; he carefully examined the cinches, latigos, stirrups; finally he checked the halter and reins. He cut a few fringes from his buckskin shirt and used them to mend a weak spot in one of his cinches. Then he saddled the Ovaro, though in fact he would be leading the sore-footed stallion much of the time.

"Then what are we going to do?" Lindy implored the moment he was done. "Just let them overtake us?"

"Eventually, yes."

Lindy paled and Newt's jaw dropped open. Fargo reached into a saddlebag and produced something wrapped in cloth.

"Got into a poker game in Congo Square out in New Orleans a while back," he explained, unwrapping the cloth. "I was drunk and a fellow talked me into taking this in place of a five-dollar bet."

Fargo opened the cloth and Lindy stepped back, her hand flying to her mouth. "My lands, what *is* it? It looks positively evil."

Fargo grinned. "*Now* you're whistling, girl. Evil . . . let's hope it looks evil enough to save our bacon."

Lindy and Newt stared in wary fascination at the crude stick-and-dried-moss doll in Fargo's hand. It was simple, yet somehow sinister, painted with bright, odd symbols and staring out of black-button eyes.

"Meet the juju man," Fargo said. "Little African devil. A cousin to Satan or some such. It's all heap-big Creole magic called Obeah."

"You believe in that stuff, Skye?" Newt asked, still staring at the sinister doll.

Fargo laughed. "Don't matter what *I* believe. These Comanches are big on black magic, and they know about evil dolls. So we're leaving this down by our campfire for them to find."

Lindy's face brightened. "And then they'll quit following us?"

Fargo shook his head. "Not likely. Comanches don't scare easy. But it'll put their nerves on edge. Then, when they catch us, I got a little something else for them."

Newt said, "Such as . . . ?"

Fargo waved him off. He nodded toward the four captives, already hitched behind the tailgate of the wagon.

"You'll see soon enough. We best hit the trail now. And, Newt, with redskins running us to ground those prisoners will likely make a fox play. I want you watching them close—make 'em feel loved."

*   *   *

Lindy drove the wagon team, Newt sitting in the bed with his Volcanic repeating rifle, eyes glued to the four hardcases trudging along behind. Fargo rode drag, staying to one side to avoid the billowing dust raised by the wagon. In every direction, the endless desert rolled like a barren sea, sterile mountains on the horizon.

"Avoid Los Angeles like you would a man-killing horse, Fargo," Rick Cully called back to him. "Big crusader like you? Son, when they get done, you'll hafta be buried with a rake."

"He won't even get there," Coyote scoffed, rolling his head to indicate the dust cloud rising closer and closer behind them.

"You boys are real witty," Fargo replied. "Way I figure it, you ought to share it with others. So about a half hour before those Comanches close for the kill, I'm gonna cut you four loose and leave you in the trail all trussed up. That should give them something to play with while we escape."

It really was a smart plan. Not sure if he meant it, all four thugs quieted down. Fargo chucked up his slightly limping Ovaro and rode up beside Lindy, who didn't see him coming. He studied her pretty but careworn face.

Fargo had been watching pilgrims for years, and he'd seen that expression plenty. They always set off with a brisk and cheerful readiness to face the future. That quickly began to crumble, replaced by a hopeless desolation as they discovered the real frontier. Fargo was sympathetic: he had roamed the American West from youth and knew both its risks and pleasures. For greenhorns, though, it was appalling.

Lindy spotted him and smiled bravely. "Any chance we'll see buffalo?"

She was only making conversation to mask her fear. But bookish Newt leaped on that one.

"No such thing as 'buffalo' out here, sis," he pontificated. "It's bison, properly."

Fargo laughed. "Buffalo, bison, big shaggy . . . hell, you'll find old bones as far east as Ohio and Kentucky. Now they're only on the western Plains, and dwindling fast. Doubt they ever made it across this desert or even tried. No grass."

"How close are the Comanches?" Lindy asked, her voice a little breathless.

"I notice you won't look back yourself," Fargo replied. "Because you might have to see the prisoners too, right?"

The Ovaro suddenly whickered, bothered by something out ahead on the trail. They had already entered the top of the long mountain pass, which wound mile after mile down toward the coast.

Fargo thumbed the riding thong off the hammer of his Colt, then loosened the Henry in its boot.

They rattled through an elbow bend. "Jesus," Newt said softly. "Is that what I *think* it is?"

Fargo said nothing, his mouth a firm, determined slit as they rolled closer to the abomination lying in the trail. The smell, in this desert heat, was ripe.

"Mail rider," he said, recognizing the leather satchel.

Thanks to carrion birds, coyotes, and desert heat, little else was recognizable. The face and skull had been beaten to a bloody pulp with stone war clubs. Not only were there a dozen arrows in his chest, but his steel picket pin had been stomped through his testicles. Even the four killers tied to the wagon were stunned into silence.

"It's barbaric," Lindy managed before looking away. "How can human beings do this to each other, Skye?"

Fargo shook his head in mute frustration. When he'd first begun yondering out west, things were different. Indians still killed whites, of course, but they used to be *proud* to kill such a worthy enemy. So they rarely abused corpses. As they had lost their respect for the white man, corpse mutilations grew widespread.

"What tribe, Skye?" Newt finally asked.

"One quick way to tell," Fargo said, swinging down from the saddle.

Some of the arrows had pierced the body through. Frowning at the distasteful contact, Fargo rolled the body over with one foot. His hunch was confirmed.

"Arrow points made of white man's sheet iron," he said, realizing full well what that meant. "A flint or obsidian arrow point ain't that hard to remove if you're patient. But sheet iron warps the moment it hits, and it clinches hard to bone. Damn near impossible to get out. And the tribe most known for their use are the Comanches."

"But they're behind us," Newt pointed out, sending a nervous glance toward that cloud of dust.

"Yeah, now they are. But this man's been dead at least a week, maybe even ten days. I'd say they passed this way on a raid down into Hermosillo, Mexico, a place they like to hit for women to sell to the Comancheros back in their home range. Now they're headed east again."

"Only after they kill you and top your woman," Cully spoke up. "Then *she* gets sold into slavery, too."

"You think they'll spare you, Cully, just because you're a low-crawling criminal? You're a white man—if they decide to attack, you'll be screaming for the next three days. All four of you will."

Fargo had no shovel, so he dragged the body off the trail and heaped rocks over it.

"How close are the Comanches now, Skye?" Lindy whispered as they resumed their slow journey through the San Bernardino Pass.

"Lots closer," he admitted. "I think they've already found our camp. Not to mention their dead scout."

"Means they should have found that creepy juju doll by now," Newt said. "You *sure* that whatever you've got in your saddlebag will scare them off?"

Fargo gave a mirthless laugh at that one. "*Sure?* With this tribe the only thing I'm *sure* of is that we'll all be damn lucky if we don't end up roasting over a torture fire."

5

The morning sun rose higher in a clear, cloudless sky of bottomless blue. The wagon creaked and rattled through the downward-spiraling pass, the mountain slopes above them growing greener and greener as the group descended toward the rainfall belt of the coast. Now and then, in momentary glimpses, they spotted the fertile plain below and the shimmering blue Pacific Ocean beyond it.

Even with all hell about to erupt, Fargo took time to appreciate the impressive view. All this scenic beauty, however, was wasted on Newt and Lindy. Both of them were pale and grim-faced, wondering how the hell Fargo could seem so nonchalant—which he wasn't. But Fargo couldn't ask greenhorns to be tough if *he* was a nervous Nellie.

"They're awfully close now, aren't they, Skye?" Lindy asked from the wagon seat.

Fargo, knowing his group couldn't run anyway, had been leading the Ovaro to ease the stallion's sore hooves. He knelt quickly to feel the ground with three fingertips.

"Be on us in about twenty minutes," he predicted, and even the prisoners looked scared.

"God protect us," Lindy prayed quickly.

Fargo doubted divine intervention was forthcoming. The great westward migration of the 1840s had encountered very little Indian trouble. By the fifties, however, Indian curiosity and amusement gave way to anger, and it sure's hell wasn't God's fault.

"Skye?" Newt said.

"Hmm?"

"Let's say that whatever trick you've got up your sleeve

41

doesn't work. Would we have any chance at all if we jus
surrendered?"

Fargo snorted. "And you claim you read up on Indians'
Newt, 'surrender' ain't in the red man's vocabulary. The
notion is cowardly to them. I've seen what happens to fool
who try it—they die even harder."

"If they capture my sister . . . ," Newt said, then chick
ened out and left the thought unfinished.

"They won't capture her," Fargo said confidently.

He said nothing else, but Fargo knew the grim facts. A
horrible as it would be for a male captive of the Coman
ches, it was infinitely worse for an attractive young woman
Every frontier veteran understood the unwritten order o
the West—better to kill a woman with a shot to the bac
of her head than let Comanches seize her.

"Fargo!" Cully shouted, his voice tight with fear. "Boy
them goddamn savages are close enough to spit on us! Yo
gotta at least untie us and give us our weapons. This ain'
right, just lettin' us get slaughtered like hogs."

"Pipe down, you jay," Fargo retorted.

"Like hell! Give us our guns, you numskull!! We ca
mount a stand with six of us."

"There'll be no shooting," Fargo assured him. "I don'
waste my time on plans that can't work."

Which didn't mean, Fargo realized nervously, that hi
alternative scheme would work either. Just then h
glimpsed the first Comanche riders above and behind ther
in the pass.

"Listen to me," he commanded the others. "I know it'
hard, but *do not* show fear. Look bored and tired, that'
all. Feel free to insult them."

Lindy gasped. "*What?* Insult wild Indians?"

"Not you, they won't take guff from a woman. But the
admire a trapped man who shows sass."

An arrow suddenly thwacked into the tailgate, just miss
ing Cully. Fargo told Lindy to rein in.

"They're not attacking, just telling us to stop. That's cau
tious, for them. Tells me they could be unnerved by tha
juju doll we left in camp. Let's hope so."

Fargo waited beside the trail, his hand on the Ovaro'
bridle to calm him as the Comanche raiding party move
cautiously closer, unsure what manner of white men thes

were. Fargo estimated about fifty riders, their half-wild mustangs painted with bright hailstone designs. The braves were typical Comanches, small and homely with clay-colored skin cured to leather by the Southwest sun of their homeland east of here.

The apparent leader, resplendent in a bone breastplate and scarlet sash, rode forward by himself, a Mexican carbine in one hand.

"Who speaks for you?" he demanded, gazing in confusion at the four prisoners. Fargo noticed, however, how his eyes lit up as he studied Lindy. Her blond hair especially intrigued him.

"I do," Fargo replied calmly. "And you would be wise to put more respect in your tone, Quohada. I am one who lives by the night."

The brave was doubly startled. First, that Fargo recognized the clan notching on his feather as the Quohada, or Antelope Eaters, band of the Comanches—few whites knew this. More shocking still, this tall, hair-face white claimed to live by the night, meaning that he was an evil *brujo* or witch.

"I lick no man's moccasins," the brave asserted, though with less contempt in his tone. "Clearly you are a brave man. You did not run from us, and even now you stand tall. This is courage! Give us the girl as tribute, and the rest of you go free."

"She's not a girl," Fargo said. "She is my squaw."

"A trifling fact! Then I will purchase her as you did."

Fargo shook his head. "No. Do not anger me, Quohada, or I will trap your spirit in a stone. I was trained by the Navajos in the secrets of the Witchery Way."

The brave's anger warred with his fear. Every Indian with brains feared Navajo black magic. He pointed his carbine at the well-armed warriors behind him.

"You see them? *No* man goes free unless he pays tribute," the Comanche insisted. "Give us your squaw."

Fargo felt his stomach ice over when all the Comanches raised their weapons, ready to cut loose.

"Tribute?" Fargo repeated. "Perhaps first you might like to meet the last red man who tried to exact tribute from me?"

Looking smug and confident, but feeling plenty nervous, Fargo opened a saddlebag and reached inside. He grabbed the second object that he had won in that New Orleans poker game—an object he had shown to few people, it was unnerving to behold.

"Here he is," Fargo said, tossing the object to the Comanche.

By force of reflex the brave caught it, and for a moment Fargo's heart sank when there was no evident reaction. However, that was only because the Comanche didn't realize, at first, what the hell this queer object was.

Then, in slow, horrified stages he recognized that he was holding a hideous, long-haired, wrinkled-up human head somehow shrunken to the size of a man's fist.

"Yiii-eee-*yah*!"

Shrieking in abject fright, the leader tossed the head aside as if it were red hot. Then he whirled his pony around and tore off without even remembering his men. They, too, caught fright and bolted off to the east.

"Deception!" Newt repeated, clapping Fargo on the back. "Skye, you're brilliant!"

"And brave," Lindy added.

Even Cully, in his great relief, joined in. "Fargo, you're some pumpkins, boy! Good work!"

Fargo felt plenty relieved too. Among other unpleasantness, he had dreaded the prospect of killing Lindy, even to save her from a life of rape and degradation. As they resumed their trek downward to the coast, Fargo began to worry anew. If Los Angeles hadn't improved recently, and was still the lawless hellhole he knew, arriving there with a beautiful woman and four hardened criminals in tow might be even riskier than facing down wild Comanches.

The sun tracked higher, and the temperature dropped pleasantly, as Fargo and his motley group descended the long mountain pass. Finally, by late afternoon, they emerged down on the plain.

"We made it!" Newt whooped. "Safe at last!"

"*Safe*, my sweet aunt," Fargo scoffed. "We're just trading red devils for white. Speaking of which . . ."

Fargo reached over and snatched off Newt's cylindrical plug hat, tossing it beside the trail.

"Hey!" Newt protested. "I bought that conk cover brand-new back in Saint Louis. Cost me three dollars."

Fargo grunted. "You bought a coffin. Plug hats like yours are favorite shooting targets out here. They symbolize the New York land speculators, and locals will fire at one on sight. They don't worry about missing the skull inside it, either."

"Jesus," a chastened Newt said. "See why we need Skye to get us to San Francisco, sis?"

"Yes, we . . . need him," Lindy agreed with a little smile, her eyes meeting Fargo's to emphasize the word *need*.

"I'll find you a reliable guide," Fargo promised.

"Yeah, Fargo, but *you* never charge the ladies a stud fee," Cully spoke up from behind.

Fargo was done playing ring-around-the-rosy with these criminal vermin.

"Cully, you'll get no water tonight," Fargo said without even slewing around in the saddle. "Keep running your mouth and you'll get no food, either."

The prisoners muttered to each other, but quieted down after that.

"How much longer to Los Angeles, Skye?" Lindy asked.

"We'll need to make one more camp. We should arrive by late morning tomorrow."

Newt had just cheered their arrival on the "safe" coastal plain. But only a half hour or so later they drew up beside a pile of sun-bleached human bones at the foot of an umbrella-shaped eucalyptus tree. A crude wooden sign had been nailed to the tree over the bones: NOUS SOMMES TOUTS SAUVAGES.

Fargo thought it might be French but couldn't read the lingo. Lindy translated it: "We are all savages."

"Truer words and all that," Newt said.

Fargo glanced at the four prisoners tied together, a vicious bunch of murdering curs.

"Maybe," he said to Newt. "But some of us are more savage than others."

"Preciso," Joaquin Robles goaded. "And even more savages in the City of Angels, *verdad*?"

Fargo picked a pleasant campsite in a copse of poplar trees beside a quick-moving stream. The night was uneventful, but the four hardcases kept Fargo and Lindy from slipping away to "pick flowers." Each time she tried to leave

45

camp, they began howling like wolves, embarrassing he
and pissing off Fargo.

They reached Los Angeles by midafternoon, and Fargo':
first glimpse was not encouraging. Despite his hopes fo
improvement, the place was still an indolent, dusty, water
starved hellhole, squalid and colorless, with neither gras
nor trees. And plenty of flyblown saloons and cantinas, bu
no mercantiles, harness shops, blacksmiths or barbershops
There was, however, a thriving undertaker's parlor, Farg•
noted—probably the first business in town after the saloons

"Not only is there a hell," Newt remarked to his sister
"but looks like we just found it."

"Bad as it looks here," Fargo warned both of them, "Sa•
Francisco is worse. You need to fight shy of that place
Believe me, I've been there."

There was a new addition since Fargo's last visit: a•
adobe-mud gate at the main entrance of the city. A two
pound howitzer was mounted atop the arch. Fargo sent •
an ominous glance—it was likely to be loaded with coppe
slugs, a lethal favorite around here.

"Nobody manning it," Newt remarked, seeing Fargo giv•
the gun a long size-up.

"A minute's notice," he replied, "can change all that."

"My God," Lindy whispered. "Look at all the me•
watching us like we're a stage act—and I don't *believe* th•
guns! Most have several, and at least one knife."

Fargo didn't bother glancing toward the men lounging o•
the rammed-earth sidewalks, most of them hip-cocked agains
buildings. Eye contact led to trouble in places like this.

"Most of these dough bellies in town," he replied
"couldn't hit a bull in the butt with a banjo. That's wh•
they have to arm themselves like express guards."

Despite his apparent apathy, however, Fargo had indee•
carefully studied the drifters and riffraff now staring at them
At least one was no local dough belly—a hatchet-faced ma•
wearing the cutaway holster of a professional gunman. N•
surprisingly, he showed a special interest in Lindy.

"Locate the marshal's office?" Newt asked.

Fargo pointed to a lot, up on their right, heaped wit•
charred wood.

"Hell, Fargo," Cully's voice jeered, "shoulda asked u•

We'da told you how that federal star packer was cut down n the street and local roughs tore his jailhouse down."

"And there is the reason why," Robles added. He pointed with his chin to a large broadsheet announcing a new no-gun ordinance. It was bullet-riddled.

Several dodgers posted nearby caught Fargo's eye. He reined in and swung down, ignoring the hostile men staring at him from lidded eyes. Among the wanted dodgers he found cluttering the wall was a group handbill with good likenesses of all four of his prisoners. They were wanted in San Francisco for crimes ranging from robbery and murder to kidnapping and rape. Each thug was worth a whopping five-hundred-dollar reward—dead or alive.

"Well, look-a-here, chappies," said the flint-eyed, hatchet-faced man who dressed like a professional killer. He nodded at Fargo. "It's the last mountain man! Guess them buckskins must mean he's hell on two sticks. Where's your mule and Hawken gun, Uncle Dick?"

Fargo ignored him and the mocking, bootlicking laughter the man's remark caused.

"So you boys *are* on the dodge," Fargo remarked as he returned to the street and swung up into leather again. "And worth two thousand dollars, huh? No wonder you been keeping your faces down since we hit this roach pit."

"So the hell what?" Cully retorted. "As you can see, ain't no 'authority' you can turn us over to in Los Angeles. You want that money, Fargo, you'll hafta haze us four all the way up to 'Frisco. So why'n'cha just spring us now and we'll pay you the reward? It's chicken feed to us."

Murder, kidnapping, rape . . . Fargo shook his head. "In a pig's ass I'll let you go. You jokers got a date with the hangman."

Newt let loose a whoop. "So you *will* take us to San Francisco?"

"Just hold your horses. I ain't conned it over yet. I might just shoot these bastards."

Fargo studied the dreary California settlement, amazed at how little it had progressed over time—had, in fact, degenerated. More than one man wore boots held together with burlap strips. A few malnourished young mothers, some of mixed Mexican and Indian blood, carried babies in flour-sack dia-

47

pers. Solid building materials were scarce, and roofing was as simple as old vegetable cans flattened into "shingles."

"My *lands,*" Lindy complained, holding a handkerchie to her nose. "The *odor.*"

Fargo knew she was too feminine to use the better wor *stink.* The town's wretched sanitation wrinkled Fargo' nose, too. Another mark against these damned cities. He' wager that sewage-infested water killed more souls than di armed conflict. Mad dogs were still on the rampage, too— Fargo could hear them snarling, a street or two over, wit an occasional gunshot silencing one.

They slowly rolled down the wide, dusty main stree Fargo watching for a boardinghouse.

"Skye?" Newt said quietly. "I know by now that you ar no coward. So why'd you let that street tough back ther insult you?"

"First of all," Fargo replied, eyes staying in careful m tion, "he *didn't* insult me although he thought he was. H called me a 'mountain man' and 'Uncle Dick.' The moun tain men were the best men America ever produced, an Uncle Dick Wootton one of the best among 'em."

Fargo inclined his head toward some of the hardscrabbl men watching them. "And second, it wouldn't've been a fi fight. Around here men assert their authority with their weap ons, not their fists. It would've been a gunfight with wome and kids caught in the crossfire. Besides . . . me and M Cutaway Holster will be locking horns later. He wasn't i sulting me, he was goading me into a cartridge session."

Lindy's fluid green eyes widened. "A gun battle wit you? But why? Skye, you just now rode into town."

Fargo glanced over at her from horseback. "Good que tion, innit? I'd say he wants me out of the way. Could b he wants you. But I'm thinking it ain't lust—it's got som thing to do with your all-fired desperation to be in Sa Francisco by November first."

"Preposterous," Lindy said, flushing a bit.

Fargo noticed the hired gun was walking slowly alon following their progress. He had the flat, reptilian eyes a cold-blooded killer, and men parted before him like wate before a ship's bow. The Trailsman knew they'd be tradin lead soon enough. His only question was *why?*

Lindy was forced to swerve the team several times—av

gamblers played dice in the street with notched beaver teeth. Even as Fargo watched, one pulled a long, narrow-bladed Arkansas toothpick just like Fargo's own, using it to slice open the hand of a man who reached in too soon for the pot.

"Hey, boys!" the trouble-seeking gunman yelled from the dirt sidewalk. "Watch buckskin boy there! He's down from the mountains and tough as a two-bit steak!"

Men laughed, including the hardcases hitched to the wagon.

"I know that gun-thrower, Fargo," Cully called out. "His name's Danford Jones. Ring a bell?"

It did indeed. Fargo knew of Jones as a notorious hired gun who worked for the lawless elements in San Francisco. He had forty kills to his credit, mostly men he goaded into drawing against him. Why was he down here in a desolate town like this when San Francisco was the center of the state's moneymaking opportunities?

"Good Lord, look what's coming," Lindy almost whispered.

Fargo had already noticed a few *nymphs du pave* walking the streets and flashing their trademark red petticoats. Now two of these sparkling doxies were strolling over to meet the occupants of the wagon.

"Howdy, you tall drink of water," a pretty redhead greeted Fargo from behind a fan. "They call me Smooth Bore."

"I am called Tit Bit," said a dusky-eyed Mexican beauty with a straining bodice to belie her name. "We are both *muy* lonely."

Lindy's nostrils flared. "Well, *he's* not . . . ladies. Good day."

"High-hatting bitch," Smooth Bore flung behind her as they left. "Bet she's frigid."

Newt, his eyes still red and watery from the journey, protested. "Hey, sis! *I'm* lonely!"

"Don't worry. I doubt they're difficult to 'engage,'" Lindy retorted. "Just toss two bits into the mud."

"Those two will eat you alive, Newt," Fargo warned.

The youth grinned and nodded. "Yeah, that's what I was hoping."

Lindy cleared her throat. Fargo laughed, then changed the subject.

"This looks like our only bet," he said doubtfully as they passed the town's only three-story building, an adobe *casa de huespedes,* or boardinghouse, from the Spanish days.

It sat in the middle of a barren sandlot, no grass or trees in sight. The Mexican owner was friendly and spoke good English. Fargo tucked a few extra silver coins into the man's palm, eliminating any objections about the seedy-looking prisoners. Fargo rented the only two remaining rooms, adjacent to each other, and herded the surly prisoners upstairs.

"You boys get a room to yourself," Fargo explained as he tied each man's hands and feet securely. "There's only two beds, but you can cozy up to each other and trade lice."

"We're hungry," Cully whined. "And I need tobacco and a sup of whiskey—"

"They want holidays in hell, too," Fargo cut him off. "You'll get fed, so quit bellyaching. But nix on the whiskey and tobacco. I'm damned if I'll mollycoddle woman killers. Not to mention that you tried to plug me."

"We didn't kill that woman—"

Fargo cut him off brusquely. "No, but you were trying your damndest. And I'd bet my horse you've killed 'em before this. You'd poleax your own mothers for a dime."

"Killed mine for nothing," Coyote interjected, and Fargo had to steel himself when he looked at that grinning face and flint-chip eyes. Robles and Cully burst out laughing, but Stone Lofley remained bored and mute.

"Eat shit, crusader!" Cully snapped behind him as Fargo headed for the door. "The worm will turn for you, boy, real soon like. Danford Jones is meaner than Satan with a sunburn, and he *will* put a few leaks in you."

Fargo paused, then turned to study Cully thoughtfully. "You seem pretty sure of that. Friend of yours, is he?"

"Never said that. I just know of him."

"Do you 'know' of Lindy Helzer and her brother, too?"

Cully's eyes cut to the rough plank floor. "You been nibbling peyote? Women like her fart through silk. How would *I* know sweet-lavender types like them?"

"Good question," Fargo said as he left the room, still frowning. "How would you?"

6

There was a cruddy bathhouse out behind the boarding-house, but in this water-scarce hovel a tub of brackish ditch water cost one dollar—fifty cents more than the bed. All three travelers had a bath, Fargo keeping his weapons close and his ears open.

The Trailsman knew damn well he couldn't leave Lindy or Newt alone in a criminal's roost like Los Angeles. There were decent people here, he'd spotted a few, but they spent most of their time hiding. Any town needed a badge-toter—this one required several, armed with double-ten express guns.

Fargo and his new trail friends walked to the town's only livery stable, a ramshackle wooden building starting to cave in on itself. Fargo led his Ovaro, Newt the team horses, two sturdy sorrels.

"Feed and a rubdown for all three," Fargo told the hos-tler, a grizzled old-timer with a peg leg. "Crushed barley if you've got it."

The old salt shook with silent laughter. "Crushed barley, uh? Son, does your mother know you're out? We're lucky we got oats in this hellhole."

He fell silent and felt the Ovaro's muscles with an expert hand. "Fella, this stallion is right outta the top drawer. Good stud. Sell him?"

"Can't. He mounts, all right, but he can't sire," Fargo lied, for he was sick of eager bidders pestering him about the Ovaro.

Fargo still hoped, if possible, to get those four rat-bastard hardcases off his hands. He asked the hostler if there was any form of law in town he could turn them over to.

"*Had* some. A good sort, U.S. Marshal Cal Richardson. But it was too much wickedness for one man to conquer. He got kilt 'bout three weeks back—hacked to death with an ax. Since then, this place has gone to hell on a fast horse. I was you folks, I'd hit the breeze, pronto."

The hostler gave them directions to the sole eating house in town that didn't serve roaches in the food. Lindy pouted when she learned the only vegetables were potatoes and onions, but a pleasantly surprised Fargo enjoyed a veritable feast of cornpone and back ribs. They washed it down with tall glasses of cold applejack—an impressive spread in a city without one icehouse or even a springhouse to keep food cool and fresh.

"Say," Newt remarked, glancing out a flyspecked window. "Look across the street—it's that man who was trying to goad you earlier. He's staring in this direction."

Fargo had already spotted Danford Jones, the hired gun thrower. "That's how it's done with these hired jobbers. Outright murder is too risky, might be a hidden witness. So they rowel a man into pulling steel in front of witnesses, then kill him in self-defense, as the law sees it."

Lindy looked troubled. "He's a hired killer?"

Fargo wiped his mouth with a linen napkin and discreetly belched. "Hell yes. They stand out like bedbugs on a clean sheet. And it looks like he's been paid to kill me."

"But . . . that's not fair! It's me who—"

Newt cleared his throat. "Clean your plate, sis. Hot meals are rare these days."

"You two take the prize," Fargo said with a sigh. "Maybe when I'm bleeding to death, you'll reveal your big secret?"

He grabbed a bundle of roast beef sandwiches he'd ordered for the prisoners. Tough, longhorn beef with little flavor and plenty of gristle, but Fargo felt it was still better than they deserved. They deserved gruel twice a day, but gruel wouldn't sustain them for the three-hundred-eighty-five-mile forced march ahead of them.

"Hey, buckskin boy!" the killer shouted as soon as Fargo emerged into the glare. "What kind of female poltroon *are* you? You got a barking iron strapped to you, yet you let a man openly insult you. You belong back east at a cider party with the rest of the sissy-bitches."

Fargo sent a sweeping glance around. The street was crowded, especially with children playing.

"C'mon," he said calmly to his companions. "This ain't the time nor place."

"You're a goddamn, gutless coward, Fargo! And your mother was a whore! I've met Indians who poked her."

Fargo grinned at his companions. "They use that line every time, too, these hired-out killers. That schoolboy claptrap is s'posed to make me see red and draw on him. It's amazing how many men take that hook."

A second later, however, a gunshot split the silence of the hot, lazy afternoon. Fargo's low-crowned hat spun off his head.

"Now he's getting personal," Fargo conceded.

Quicker than eyesight, Fargo's Colt leaped into his fist. The first shot knocked Jones' hat off his head, but unlike Fargo's it didn't hit the ground right away. Fargo emptied his Colt, and each bullet kept the hat flying and jerking through the air like a kite with no tail. He sent it a half block away—and then caused a collective gasp of astonishment when he dropped it perfectly on the head of a lounging townie. That landing was sheer accident, but only Fargo knew it.

Several spectators cheered and applauded openly while Fargo thumbed reloads into his Colt. Danford Jones looked like a man who had been punched hard, but not quite dropped.

"C'mon," Fargo urged his companions. "We've got one more stop."

Jones, no man to be publicly buffaloed, shouted after them in his bullhorn voice: "Real pretty shooting, Uncle Dick! But *killing* ain't so easy and pretty! Take a good gander around you—you've seen your last town and your *last* sunrise."

One more task remained—stocking up on provisions for the trail. Fargo still hoped to dispose of his prisoners and report to his new employer, the Pacific & Western Railroad, whose offices were located just north of here in tiny Santa Paula. He had a sinking feeling, however, that he would instead be going to San Francisco against his will—although, if so, a two-thousand-dollar reward was far more than he stood to make as a guard for a surveying crew.

They managed to find only one so-called mercantile, a poorly stocked, open-fronted stall on Pacific Street. Unfortunately, even though the Sierra gold rush was in its last days, gold-camp prices still applied to packaged groceries.

"Christ on a crutch!" Newt exclaimed, pointing to a stack of tin cans of corn and peas. "Three dollars per can! They're about thirty cents back in Illinois."

"Only thing cheap out west is human life," Fargo remarked, watching Danford Jones, who still shadowed them. Since Fargo's shooting demonstration, he had kept a respectful distance.

Hardtack, dried fruit, and raw beans traveled well; they were also less expensive, so the trio stocked up on all three.

They returned to their shared room. It was rustic but reasonably clean, with only two narrow iron bedsteads topped by corn-husk mattresses. The poverty of Los Angeles was apparent in the crude skunk-oil lamps with rag wicks.

Fargo stayed with the prisoners long enough to untie their hands and let them eat, his cocked Colt on them at all times.

"Fargo," Rick Cully cajoled around a mouthful of tough beef, "why be a damn fool? Ain't nobody needs to kill you if you just let us four go and quit wet-nursin' them pilgrims. They can make it to 'Frisco on their own."

"Sure, and oysters can walk upstairs. Why were you boys hired to douse their lights, and who paid you?"

Cully only shook his head. "It's your ass, Fargo. I tried to wise you up. Whatever happens now is your own goddamn stupid fault."

When Fargo returned to the room, Newt was reading an old newspaper and Lindy was gazing at a tintype.

"That's a good likeness of you," Fargo remarked, glancing over her shoulder.

"It's not me, Skye. It's my twin sister, Belinda."

"Sorry to hear she died so young."

Lindy's nostrils flared. "Died? Dying is a natural thing. But Belinda—"

Newt coughed a warning and Lindy fell silent.

"I see I'm smack in the middle of another damn mare's nest," Fargo grumped, "with no end in sight."

Newt sat up in bed and swung his feet to the floor. "The way you're complaining," he said hopefully, "sounds like you'll be taking us up north?"

"That's not set in stone," Fargo replied. "But it might be necessary if I want to see those four hardcases jugged and collect the reward."

"But can we get there by November first, Skye?" Lindy implored. "That's less than two weeks from now."

"Or else you lose your boardinghouse, right?" he said sarcastically. "Well, it's 385 miles to San Francisco. The Old Mission Trail hugs the coast and goes as far north as the Santa Cruz Mission, just about sixty miles south of 'Frisco. There's a freight road the rest of the way."

"But can we make it *in time*?" Lindy repeated.

Skye, busy unbuckling his heavy leather gun belt, shrugged one shoulder. "We'd have to make maybe thirty miles a day to get there on time. Granted, the coast road is pretty good, and a horsebacker could cover it in jig time. We *might* be able to do it with your conveyance and those four maggots walking behind. I wouldn't give odds on it with only a two-horse team. Besides, I'm more worried about road bandits than making good time—they favor the coast."

It was only early evening, and the setting sun blazed in the windows, but all three travelers had seen little sleep in the past two days.

"Well," Newt said, yawning, "what about the sleeping arrangements? There's three of us and only two beds."

Lindy cast a seductive gaze at Fargo, perhaps suggesting they could share. The Trailsman, however, well versed in amorous matters, reluctantly dismissed that tempting arrangement. A corn-husk mattress was fairly comfortable, but rustled every time the sleeper moved. He was no prude, but making mad, rustling love to a girl in the presence of her brother held little appeal for Fargo.

"You and me will switch off on sentry duty," Fargo told Newt. "So we'll also take turns with the bed. With Danford Jones on the prowl, and four killers next door, we're double-barreled fools if we don't post a guard. I'll take the first shift."

55

* * *

Fargo's biggest problem was the struggle to stay awake.

He had pulled a ladder-back chair out into the hallway with a clear view of both doors. He sat with his Henry across his thighs and his Colt hanging on the chair near to hand. The serious threat of fire meant no lamps could be burned unattended, and only ghostly moonlight illuminated the hallway.

To stay awake Fargo tried walking back and forth. Even though the floorboards creaked with a terrible racket, he was soon nodding out on his feet. In desperation he resorted to a trick he'd learned from an old army scout—Fargo dug a twist of chewing tobacco from his possible bag and got it juicing good. Then he pulled back each eyelid and smeared some juice on them. Although harmless, the juice would lightly sting the eyes for hours, especially when closed.

Now and then Fargo left his corner of the upstairs landing for a wider patrol. He noticed there were plenty of doors and windows, and the locks were notoriously easy to pick.

Newt took the second shift, then roused Fargo at midnight. Even this late Los Angeles stayed wild and raucous, with gunshots and drunken shouts peppering the night.

"Any problems?" Fargo asked, yawning.

"Nah, but this place has got rats long as your arm," Newt complained. "I damn near stepped on one."

"'Rats' is just the word," Fargo said grimly as he pulled on his boots. "Speaking of which . . . any trouble from next door?"

Newt shook his head. "Door's still locked and there's no noises except snoring. Jesus, they sound like threshing machines."

"One thing about the worst criminals," Fargo said, palming the wheel of his Colt, "they always sleep like babies. Amazing what you can do without a conscience."

"Thanks for keeping the bed warm," Newt said, yawning, as he crawled under the blanket.

Fargo turned toward the door and spotted Lindy, wide awake in the blue-tinged moonwash. Her sensuous mouth formed a pout. The little imp had decided to tease him—

or else she was reminding him what was available to him any old damn time.

She had worn a simple linen sacque to bed, but now it was rolled up to her neck. Hot blood exploded into his shaft when he saw that slender, trim-waisted, full-breasted, pale ivory body. Even as Fargo stared, his pulse pounding like Pawnee war drums, she tweaked her plum-colored nipples until they were hard and pointy.

She crooked a finger, inviting him into her bed.

Fargo, caught between duty and desire, felt himself weakening.

A sudden thump out in the hallway called him back to duty.

Fargo jacked a round into the Henry's chamber, then eased through the door into the moonlit hallway. He slipped a skeleton key into the lock of the prisoners' door and quietly eased it open. Nothing seemed amiss—each bed held two men, all four snoring with a racket like boars in rut. Fargo checked the windows, but the latches were all closed.

"That thump was just one of the guests slamming his door," Fargo muttered as he locked the door.

Nonetheless, Fargo had not survived hundreds of scrapes by making easy assumptions. For the next ten minutes or so he prowled every corridor on the second and third floors, checking each hallway window. All seemed secure.

The Trailsman returned to his chair on the top floor and resumed his lonely vigil. He thought, for a moment, that he heard faint whispering sounds from the prisoners' room, but the wind in the eaves made the same sound.

Still . . . something nagged at him, that inner voice that had warned him, so many times before, of lethal danger.

But *what* was bothering him? He suddenly understood when Newt's words echoed in memory: *Jesus, they sound like threshing machines.*

The riotous snoring, once clearly audible through the door, had stopped.

"Here's the fandango," Fargo told himself, pushing out of his chair.

He walked on his heels to minimize the noise. When Fargo reached out and pushed on the door with three fingertips, it eased open an inch. A candle burned inside, its weak light dancing on the rose-pattern wallpaper. Since he'd locked the door barely ten minutes ago, that meant the intruder must have picked the lock, or used his own skeleton key, while Fargo was patrolling the house.

Fargo banged open the door, his Henry preceding him into the room. Danford Jones, face sinister and chiseled in the dim light, was in the act of untying Rick Cully. A bulging burlap sack sat by the open window, and one end of a rope had already been tied to a leg of one of the beds, with the other dangling out the window.

"You don't want to come between a dog and his meat, Danford," Fargo said calmly. "These owlhoots are mine."

"Sure, Fargo," the killer said, standing up slowly. "I was hoping to turn them in myself, but you caught me."

Fargo knew Jones was dangerous, but before he could order him to surrender his six-gun the man moved quicker than a striking snake. In a move he must have practiced often, the gunman did a fast sidestep shuffle even as his short iron appeared in his hand like magic.

Superior reflexes had pulled Fargo's bacon from the fire before, and he relied on them now. He dropped to the floor even as Jones' belt gun exploded the silence of the sleeping house. Slugs chewed up the door behind Fargo as he opened fire.

One of the thugs had blown out the candle, reducing Fargo's target to a dim outline. So he squeezed off round after round, aiming at muzzle flash. The acrid stench of spent powder filled the room as the grim battle heated up.

Finally, with a surprised and airy grunt, Jones flopped hard to the floor. Fargo lit the candle to make sure he was dead. Six blood-seeping holes, ranging between his stomach and chest, were Danford Jones' death certificate. Mixed with the room's burnt-powder stench was the sheared-copper odor of blood.

"Damn good shootin', Fargo!" Cully sucked up. "That bastard meant to kidnap us!"

"Yeah," Fargo retorted, tightening the man's ropes. "That's why there's gun shapes bulging out that burlap sack, right?"

"Aww, hell, we—"

A sudden female scream of terror from Fargo's room

iced over his blood. Too late he realized there were two killers!

Fargo burst into his room just in time to see a bearded man in a long gray duster struggling with Lindy, a huge bowie knife in his right hand. The plucky young woman held his arm with both hands, barely preventing him from slitting her throat. Newt, his head badly gashed, lay half-conscious on his bed.

Lindy's would-be assassin stood between her bed and the window. Fargo's slug thumped into his ample belly; he cartwheeled backward, lost his balance, and shattered the windowpane as he fell three stories to the sandlot below.

"Take care of your brother!" Fargo shouted before he raced downstairs and past the cowering owner. He hoped to interrogate that man if he still had life in him after the fall.

The intruder did, but just barely. Fargo's slug would have killed him eventually, gutshots almost always being fatal, but the thug had broken his neck in the fall and was only minutes from death.

"Who hired you?" Fargo demanded. "You're going to glory now, mister, so might's well clear the slate."

Blood trickled over the man's beard-stubbled chin. "I work for . . . *Christ* that hurts! Work for . . . Wagner."

A coughing spasm wracked the dying man's body. Fargo became aware that a crowd was rapidly gathering— including several well-armed men with hostile faces. *After all,* Fargo reminded himself, *I'm a stranger and this pond scum is a local.*

"Wagner?" Fargo repeated. "Is that his front name or back?"

More blood, tinged pink, frothed on the man's lips. The effort to speak made him choke.

"Leave him be, you stinkin' bastard," growled a big man wearing butternut homespun. "Griff is well liked around here."

"Yeah, he would be," Fargo agreed. "He's straight and honorable, right? Good family man?"

"None a your damn business. Can't you see he's dying?"

Fargo stood up and faced the growing crowd. He'd learned long ago never to show fear to bullyboys.

"Not only can I see he's dying," Fargo told the speaker, "but it's a reg'lar tonic to me. More like him require killing.

Now . . . a few seconds ago you called me a stinking bastard. The stinking part I'll give you, even though I had a bath. But you insulted my mother when you called me a bastard. Are you going to swallow that word back, or do me and you take a walk into the street and unlimber?''

Fargo wasn't really offended, just taking his place in the pecking order. He palmed the butt of his Colt, waiting. Just then the man on the sandy ground did indeed die. His last, long breath was expelled with a sound like pebbles rattling in a sluice gate.

The hostility eased from the butternut-clad man's face, replaced by resentful fear.

"No disrespect to your mother, stranger. It was just a manner of speaking.''

Fargo nodded. "Good enough.''

The Trailsman headed back into the house, not turning his back fully on the crowd. That insincere apology just now meant nothing, he realized. The anger over this killing was going to heat up all night—and reach a furious boil by morning.

"Leave *now*?'' Lindy exclaimed. "But, Skye . . . it's pitch-dark out there!''

"That's the point. Believe me, we won't make it out alive if we wait till morning. Someday, maybe, this snake den will become a by-God community. But right now it's just an outlaw town, and there's plenty of men here who find killing a man easier than swatting a fly.''

Fargo grabbed his saddle and bridle, preparing to hustle over to the livery and retrieve the Ovaro. Newt, too, was pulling on his boots to go with him and bring back the wagon and team. He was still pale from the blow to his head.

"Ask you two something?'' Fargo said. "Why aren't either one of you speculating as to *who* is trying to kill Lindy?''

An awkward silence followed his question.

"You yourself,'' Lindy finally replied, "told us, just now, this town is filled with killers.''

"Sure. But this one was bent on killing *you*, sugar plum, a mighty comely woman. And seems to me those four in the next room were aiming to kill you when they attacked you in the desert. That's not exactly the *first* thing most woman-starved men would do with a beauty like you—unless they were jobbers, hired killers like Jones."

"Preposterous," Lindy scoffed. She stepped behind a three-panel dressing screen to change for the trail.

"Jesus," Fargo snapped. "You two are piss-poor liars. I'd ought to toss both of you to the wolves. C'mon, Newt, let's get a wiggle on. Won't take these peckerwoods long to seal off the city."

Fargo left his Colt with Lindy, then handed her a gold cartwheel. "When you're dressed, take this downstairs to the owner."

"You've been paying all along," she pointed out. "Shouldn't we be doing that?"

"You will," Fargo assured her. "I'm keeping accounts in my head."

Both men left the house by the back door. Fargo leading, they made their way cautiously toward the livery, rifles at the ready as they moved through the inky shadows.

"Man you were right," a nervous Newt remarked, watching men rush to the few points where the city could be entered or left. "And they aren't waiting till morning."

"It'll only stir up the shit even more," Fargo told him, "when they find out Danford Jones is dead, too."

"So how do we get past them?"

"We can pray for a miracle," Fargo replied, "or get set to blast our way out."

"Cripes," Newt said, "the way *I* shoot? Lindy's right—I can't hit the inside of a tent."

"Yeah, I noticed. But you've got grit, lumberjack, and I noticed how you just stood there sassy while lead whistled in."

"Yeah, but—"

"For a hot bust out," Fargo assured him, "noise is all you need. That Volcanic you're packing holds thirty shots. Accuracy doesn't matter, these blowhards are mostly chickenshits made brave by whiskey. When I give you the high sign, just start busting caps and throw up a screen of lead."

Fortunately, the dilapidated livery was in a quiet part of town. Fargo liberated all three horses, leading them into the hoof-packed yard, where he and Newt quickly harnessed the team to the wagon. By now almost every male who was still available had gathered at the two entrances to Los Angeles, so Fargo and Newt made it back to the house unobserved.

The prisoners, led by Rick Cully, began to loudly complain about being forced to give up their sleep. Fargo had no time for it now. He snarled impatiently and adjusted their attitudes by backhanding Cully so hard his eyes crossed.

"Shut your filthy sewers," Fargo growled. "The first son of a bitch who gives me trouble will be walking with his ancestors. I've had my belly full of murdering trash like you."

Faces crimson with rage, yet eyes filled with fear of Fargo's wrath, the owlhoots made no resistance when Fargo led them downstairs and hitched them on a lead line to the tailgate of the wagon.

"Why is your stallion hitched back with the prisoners?" Newt asked when he, Fargo and Lindy were set to leave.

"I'll be driving the wagon until we clear this vermin trap," Fargo replied. "Lindy will be lying down in the back. You'll be riding shotgun messenger, and when I give the hail I want you to make that repeater bark and bark *loud*."

Fargo knocked the riding thong off the hammer of his Colt. Reins in one hand, Henry in the other, he shouted, "Gee up!" The team lurched into motion and they angled out into the wide, moonlit street.

The Trailsman held the reins back tight until the first shout of warning, from the adobe arch, told him they'd been sighted.

"Hang on tight!" he shouted, loosening the reins and roaring at the team. "Newt, hunch down and be ready!"

"Hey! *Hey,* goddamn it!" Cully protested. His legs, like those of the other prisoners, pumped furiously to keep the men from being dragged through the dust. "Slow the hell down, Fargo!"

"No, *you* hurry the hell up!" Fargo shouted back.

The first weapon opened up, orange streaks of muzzle flash marking the shooters.

"Now, Skye?" Newt shouted nervously.

"Not yet," Fargo ordered, slapping the team with the reins, "or we'll run out of ammo too soon."

Many of the shooters were drunk, and their bullets sailed

wide. Still, with scores of men firing at them, Fargo knew some lead would do damage—a few slugs were already dangerously close. Several rounds thwacked into the wagon, making Lindy cry out in fright.

By now Fargo had whipped the semirested team up to a frenzy, and the Dougherty wagon bounced crazily, almost throwing Newt off the board seat.

"Fargo, you low-down son of a bitch!" Cully shrieked, about to lose his footing as Robles, Coyote, and Stone Lofley already had. "We're being *dragged* back here!"

Fargo ignored him, not giving a damn anyway—he had just noticed, as they raced closer to the arch, that a man stood over the howitzer. The gun was aimed out of town, not toward the center.

Newt, too, saw him.

"Bleeding Christ, Skye!" he shouted. "We'll be blown to smithereens!"

Fargo flinched when a humming bullet grazed his cheek with hot pain like a razor cut.

"Make it warm up on that arch, Newt!" he shouted above the hammering racket of gunfire. "I'll concentrate on the closest shooters aiming at us. You don't have to hit your man up there, just pin him down. If that jasper gets a good bead on us with that howitzer, the trip's over."

Fargo jammed the reins into his teeth and both men opened fire, Newt upward toward the man on the arch, Fargo toward the throng blocking their path—the most immediate threat. Again and again the reliable, well-maintained Henry slapped Fargo's cheek as he emptied the sixteen-round magazine with deadly precision. After the first thug dropped hard into the dust, the rest cleared back like startled birds.

The Henry's hammer finally clicked on an empty chamber, Newt's thirty-round Volcanic still chattering. Fargo didn't hesitate a second because thugs still lined both sides of the street. He drew his Colt, fired three shots from his left hand, then did a quick border shift, tossing the gun into his right hand to empty the chambers in that direction.

Robles was closest to the tailgate and managed to regain his feet long enough to make a mighty leap, draping his upper body over it. The position was awkward but kept him from dragging.

"Hey, Fargo!" he taunted. "That howitzer does not fear famous men! This is the end of the trail, gringo *famoso*. Surrender now, or those copper slugs will tear you into trap bait, *verdad*?"

The arch was within throwing distance now. Despite emptying his entire magazine in that direction, Newt had only made the gunner flinch a few times.

"Old son, you're no Indian fighter," Fargo told Newt through grim lips. "You'd have better luck throwing something at the bastard."

Fargo, both guns empty, was only being sarcastic. A moment later, however, Newt surprised him by picking up an extra horseshoe from the wagon bed and flinging it at the man.

Fargo, lips tugging into a grin, saw him stagger and almost fall. Then, in an eyeblink, they had streaked through the gate.

With bullets dogging them, Fargo tossed the reins to Newt while he rapidly reloaded his Colt.

"We made it!" Newt whooped. "Nobody following us."

"Stay down," a worried Fargo snapped when Lindy started to sit up. "Newt didn't knock that gunner down. And we ain't out of range."

"*Mira!* Look, Fargo is afraid of a little pop gun!" Robles mocked while his three companions were still being dragged through the choking dust. " 'A legend big as the West,' yet see how he pules and trembles before a two-pounder! *Ay, mamacita!* That little toy could not—"

With an earsplitting *ka-whumpf* the howitzer finally opened up, belching smoke, sparks and a deadly load of copper slugs. A few chunked into the wagon or kicked up dust geysers around them. But most of the copper projectiles tore into the upper half of Robles' big body, and he was literally shredded to tatters in front of his horrified fellow criminals.

7

"*Damn* you to hell, Fargo!" Rick Cully screamed from the midst of a boiling dust cloud behind the wagon. "*Stop* this son of a bitch, wouldja? Christ, we're dragging through the dirt like plows. And Robles is coming apart all over us!"

Fargo, riding the Ovaro now, grinned in the dark as he reined in and slued around in the saddle to check their backtrail. Then he swung down and placed his fingers against the ground.

"We've come a few miles by now," he told Newt and Lindy. "With no pursuit that I can feel. We can slow down."

He set to work on the grisly task of cutting Robles—what was left of him—free from the lead line. Fargo dragged the sopping remains to the side of the road. The other three prisoners, too shocked and exhausted for any hot-jawing, struggled to their feet, coughing from the thick dust and trying not to retch.

"Hell," Fargo muttered, "there goes five hundred dollars right down a rat hole. I could've used his head to collect the reward. But there's not enough of it left to identify him."

Newt craned his head around to watch the trail. "Think those hardcases might form a posse?" he inquired nervously.

"Ain't likely," Fargo told him. "These are townies, like most criminals. There's damn few horses in that burg, didn't you notice? No tie rails and only one broken-down livery. I was going to suggest you buy two more team horses, but then I realized there weren't any. Raiding Indians from east of here steal most of 'em."

"Besides," Newt put in proudly, thinking of that heart-pounding escape from Los Angeles, "those bullyboys want no part of a real fight, right, Skye? And now they know they'll get one from us."

Fargo nodded. "You're a quick study, Newt. Best to take that type by the horns and throw them."

By now Rick Cully had recovered some of his usual nasty disposition.

"Holy shit, Fargo!" he exclaimed. "You're dumping Joaquin aside like a sack of garbage. Ain'tcha even gonna bury him, you pagan son of a bitch?"

"A sack of garbage, I would bury as a courtesy," Fargo said. "But I don't bury any rat bastard who tries to kill me."

He hooked a thumb over his shoulder toward the dusty pueblo and the armed mob. "You're worth five hundred dollars to them. You want to hang around here and bury Robles yourself? I'll cut you loose."

"Ahh . . ." The killer piped down, his face sulky.

Lindy was unharmed but shaken from the shooting fray and wild bouncing of the wagon. Fargo helped her onto the seat beside her brother. It was cooler down here on the coastal plain, especially at night, and she was shivering until Fargo tossed her shawl over her.

"Is the ocean close?" she asked, ready to soldier on bravely.

Fargo nodded. "My horse already smells it. We'll reach the Old Mission Trail by forenoon," he predicted. "Hugs the shoreline almost all the way up. But don't let the pretty view fool you. We won't be able to send out a scout, and unscouted country is the most dangerous anywhere. There's too many gun-handy men running loose around here."

"Straight talk, Fargo," Coyote said, his long black hair now powdered yellow-brown with dust. "It is road gangs you must worry about now. Men just like us."

"How you like them apples, cock chafer?" Cully taunted.

Fargo held up the broadsheet with its likeness of the four owlhoots. He had peeled it off the wall for just this moment.

"*You* jackasses best worry about gangs, too. If they kill me, they'll find this and realize you three are money for old rope. And, Coyote, you being a Messy"—Fargo meant

Mescalero Apache—"won't set well with any Mexer road gangs. Not after all the killing your people have done down in Old Mex."

Coyote's face closed up again. Fargo gave the prisoners a quick drink of water, then Newt chucked the team into rattling motion. The sandy trail was wide here, and Fargo rode beside the wagon. Despite the late hour he kept his gaze sweeping all around them.

However, his ears were as good as his eyes.

"Another whole day almost behind us," he overheard Lindy murmur to Newt. "Mr. Trumble said we *must* be in San Francisco by November first or it's too late."

"We'll be there, sis," Newt encouraged her.

"We *have* to be. Oh, we just have to. That monster must be stopped. But there's only ten days left."

"Now me, I don't mind stopping monsters," Fargo interjected as if he'd been invited to speak. "Never have liked 'em. But I don't much like being bamboozled into it."

An embarrassed pause as they realized Fargo overheard them. Then:

"Nobody's 'bamboozled' you, Skye," Lindy protested.

"Ah, cowplop. For starters, there's no boardinghouse in your future, is there?"

There was enough moonlight to clearly see Lindy when she finally shook her head.

"The name Wagner mean anything to you?" he pressed, recalling the dying man he'd shot in his room.

"Yes, but I'm sworn to secrecy, Skye."

"Sworn?"

Lindy nodded again, and Fargo shrugged. "All right then, if that's the way of it. An oath is an oath."

"Well, lah-dee-dah, a man of *honor*!" Cully taunted as he trudged along behind the wagon. "Hey, Fargo, make your halo glow for us!"

"If I require your opinion, cockroach," Fargo replied absently, "I'll beat it out of you."

The Trailsman's mind was already ranging to the long trip ahead, a journey fraught with more dangers than these tenderfoots could imagine in their worst nightmares. And the greatest danger of all lay at end-of-trail, the most wide-open city in the West, San Francisco.

*   *   *

"Terrible" Jack Slade spent the first part of his morning at the Plaza, San Francisco's main square, supervising the hanging of a Modoc Indian caught stealing a meat pie from a street vendor. Since the arrival of District Attorney Tom Trumble, there'd been much talk of "an honest police force." So far, however, Trumble had little influence to back his talk. So Slade's men were still swaggering it around, wearing their huge tin stars.

After the badly botched hanging, Slade heated himself to a sweat using Judge Lash to scourge several miscreants. Their crime was disrespect to the Regulators, as Slade called his set of saloon thugs. His very first lash, with the cruelly modified whip, tore a four-inch strip of flesh from a Mexican's back.

Toward noon, Slade and his boss met on Union Street.

"A telegram arrived less than an hour ago, Jack," Prescott Wagner greeted him. "Both of my men down in Los Angeles were killed, and the girl escaped. And what we suspected has been confirmed—that *is* Skye Fargo with her. Just my damn luck."

Wagner fell silent and gave a running-for-office smile to a group of passing matrons. He and Slade were strolling along Union Street's new raw-lumber boardwalk. It was only late morning, but already a steady, raucous din emanated from the infamous Barbary Coast district along the waterfront.

Slade, never easily impressed, stopped in his tracks. "Fargo killed *both* of them? Griff and Danford?"

"Dead as King Tut," Wagner confirmed emphatically.

Slade gave a low, slow whistle. Griff Weston was a cool, hardened killer formed in the bloody cauldron of the Mexican War, and Danford Jones was among the most feared shootists in all of California.

"No man could be that good," Slade said dismissively. "Fargo must have rolled a seven, that's all."

"Horseshit, my friend. Luck had nothing to do with it," Wagner insisted. "Fargo is rawhide tough, and he's smart. Worse, now he's on his way up here to *Alta California*. It's up to you now, Jack. Don't miscalculate this man, he's more than just back-country lore. Like Shadrach in the Bible, Skye Fargo always emerges miraculously alive."

Slade nodded. He was a blunt, brutal man who divided

men up into two groups: talkers and silent men, talkers being trouble. He disdained his talkative boss, but liked the wages he paid. Besides—Wagner was right. *Both* men would stretch hemp if Wagner was convicted.

"Things around here have changed somewhat since the days when this was Yerba Buena," Wagner remarked. "But the place is still a bear-and-bull pit, not a community. Sadly, statehood is changing all that. There'll be plenty more 'reformers' like Trumble nosing in."

Slade grunted agreement. "I see the mealymouthed psalm singers arriving every day now."

Wagner, his diamond belt buckle throwing off rays of reflected sunlight, surveyed the area with a proprietor's eye. He had seen many born-on-the-spot towns, but this one beat the band. The streaming crowd included platoons of drummers wearing their trademark straw boaters with brightly colored bands. The early prospectors were being edged out by deep-rock miners. They were easily recognizable by their unnaturally pale skin and clothes stained red with ore.

Chinese workers in floppy blue blouses and long pigtails hauled wooden yokes with water pails dangling from both ends. Several of these "Celestials" gazed with fear and respect at the blacksnake whip wrapped around Slade's left arm like a pet—Wagner knew many of them had felt its razor-sharp teeth. Above the city and the bay the hills had been denuded of timber for shoring up mines. Now they were chockablock with tar-papered shacks.

From the direction of Telegraph Hill came two distinct gunshots.

"Hell," Wagner remarked, "that's the Murphy-Bullock duel. I meant to take it in."

Duels in San Francisco were now so common that they were advertised in the newspapers so spectators could attend.

Even this early, and out in public, Wagner was sipping one of his beloved mint juleps. Even in almost lawless San Francisco, however, a man out on the hustings had to at least *look* respectable. So he had abandoned glass for a cup of polished black buffalo horn.

"Got a preference?" Slade asked. "How it's did, I mean?"

Both men watched the streaming crowd warily. "Provincial morality" didn't exist in wide-open San Francisco, and the city was filled with young hotheads who liked to cut up rough—the slightest accidental bump, along any street, could leave a man dead.

"A preference?" Wagner shrugged one shoulder. To get what he wanted, he always tried blandishments, cunning, and bribes first. If all that failed, there was always violence. "Anything that isn't too obvious, Jack. Attacks by road gangs are frequent along the Old Mission Trail. And never mind the prisoners or even Fargo until you've killed the woman—it's Lindy Helzer who will sink us. Sink us six feet closer to hell."

Slade nodded. "I figured me and Lumpy Neck McGuire would be hittin' the trail. So I rigged up a few little surprises for Fargo and company."

Slade dipped several blunt, callused fingers into the front pocket of his duster. Wagner stared in fascination at the four modified projectiles in Slade's palm.

"The hell *are* those?" he demanded.

"Explosive bullets. Invented them myself. I hollow out the very tip of forty-four slugs and then stick twenty-two blanks inside them."

"Blanks? Then why bother?"

On those rare occasions when he smiled, such as right now, Slade revealed liver-colored gums and teeth like two rows of crooked yellow gravestones.

"Why bother?" he repeated. "Because the twenty-two bullet ain't needed, just the full powder load in the blank. It explodes when the forty-four impacts. Makes a normal hole going in, but by the time it exits it's the size of a plum. Even a leg or arm hit is fatal because they bleed out like stuck pigs. When it hits a human head, it blows out one whole side like a melon under a hammer."

Wagner trusted his lackey when it came to matters of firearms and explosives.

"Good thinking," he praised. "Skye Fargo is known as a hard man to kill, and it's a safe bet he'll need to be snuffed out along with the Helzer girl. It's best to plant the brother, too, even though he wasn't a witness to . . . the events in Arizona Territory."

Wagner had few regrets. After all, a man had to bet big to win big. But the girl in Arizona, Lindy Helzer's twin sister—that was a mistake, if not a regret, and had to be covered up completely.

"What about Cully and them?" Slade asked. "They won't testify against you unless they're arrested. Otherwise, you won't find them near the law, not with a good price on their heads."

"You're right. They won't testify unless they're arrested. At which point they'll sing like canaries. If you and Lumpy can spring them along the trail, fine. If not . . . they'll be sacrificed for the cause."

"The cause?" Slade repeated sarcastically. "Since when we got a cause?"

Wagner smiled, sweeping out one arm to indicate the steep, teeming slopes of *his* city. "Look at it, Jack. That's our cause—perpetual wealth. Most boomtowns turn quickly into ghost towns. But San Francisco is going to avoid that fate. And you know why?"

Wagner was the type who would wait, so Slade said, "Why?"

"Because this is not a city—it's a saturnalia. And so long as it stays that way, for the two of us it's Coronado's City of Gold. Already I'm the area's real estate mandarin, and half the brewery business is mine. And it all started by acquiring a few modest gold claims."

Slade had no idea what "saturnalia" meant and didn't give a frog's fat ass. His boss was a talker, and talkers got on Slade's nerves. Hell, a bunch of *women* talked.

"It's Lindy Helzer who's the real fly in the ointment," Wagner repeated, his cold black eyes burning with murderous intent. "She came all the way out here just to testify. And Trumble, mushy-headed do-gooder that he is, is determined to use her testimony to seal his case against me. Still . . ."

He lapsed into silence for a few moments, recalling Belinda Helzer and the way her silky-satin skin had felt against his. So what if he held a gun to her head the whole time—and, afterward, silenced her for eternity with a knife to her heart?

"You know," Wagner mused aloud, "this Lindy Helzer is the spitting image of her . . . deceased sister. Very comely. If I could only—"

"Katy Christ, boss," Slade cut in, "put it out of your

thoughts. Just go to whores like I do. We got enough messes to clean up. Never mind court—if a beauty like Malinda Helzer even *arrives* in town, the whole damn story will get noised about. Stealing a claim from a Mexican, hell, that's small potatoes. But raping and killing a respectable white woman? They'll drag-hang you in the streets."

Enough messes . . . Wagner felt the bile of anger erupt up his throat. He had always been careful to conduct most of his business by "sub-rosa accord," i.e., no incriminating records. Around here, though, rumors were always thicker than toadstools after a hard rain.

Saloon gossip . . . that was how brand-new District Attorney Tom Trumble, a damned crusader like Fargo, came to indict him—including the devastating gossip about the woman killed in Arizona. He couldn't actually be tried for that crime here in California. But the testimony by Lindy Helzer could—no, *would*—be devastating.

"All this shit," Wagner complained, "was started by a goddamn nosy clerk who turned up 'deficiencies' in my early claim filings. Now I'll soon be on trial for claim-jumping and multiple murders. But, one way or the other, I'll prevent any guilty verdict. An acquittal means I'm a shoo-in for the next mayoral election."

"Prevent the verdict how?" demanded Slade as they entered the door of Wagner's offices on Sacramento Street.

"Well, the local charges don't worry me. We never killed a white man, so who cares? I've paid plenty of people *not* to care."

"Sure. But sometimes gate money don't open the gate."

"I'll know how things stand even before the trial," Wagner said while they ascended a narrow stairwell that smelled of beeswax. "And if my informants suggest things are going badly for me—perhaps there'll be another devastating fire at the courthouse. All the records and evidence would go up, too, of course."

Slade whistled. "Damn, boss! Talk about destroying the lawn to kill the crabgrass. *You* got buildings near the Plaza, too, most of them wood."

Wagner nodded, pulling a key on a gold chain from his fob pocket and unlocking the office door.

"That's why I called it a last resort," he said. "Obviously, I'm banking on you and Lumpy having success along the

Old Mission Trail. Apropos of that . . . maybe I can trump those explosive bullets of yours."

He unlocked the top drawer of his kneehole desk and slid it open carefully. Slade's brutal face was split by a grin of delight when he glanced inside at the sticks of dynamite. Fuses and crimping caps were included.

"*Hell*, yes," approved Slade, a former deep-rock miner and explosives expert. "A good part of the trail is flanked on the east by steep mountain slopes. We could practically drop it on them. I've got a few cans of blasting powder, too."

"Only if all else fails," Wagner cautioned. "Dynamite is beyond the skill of most road gangs and would look suspicious. And, if possible, I'd like to spare Cully and the others—they've done good work for me. But time is pressing—if necessary just use explosives and kill them all."

Slade nodded. He had carried out most of the killing and torture for his boss, and if Wagner went to the gallows, he was next.

"Gotcha, boss. But if I get the chance . . ."

Slade glanced down at the whip on his arm, its popper bristling with razored flint.

". . . I mean to strip Skye Fargo down to his bones."

"*If* you get the chance," Wagner agreed. "I begrudge no man his fun, and you, Jack, do dearly love to administer a good whipping. Just write this on your pillowcase: I don't want anyone testifying at that November first trial, least of all Malinda Helzer."

The morning sun was well up when Fargo's party emerged from dense tree cover and reached the Old Mission Trail established by the Spanish *padres*. The Santa Barbara Channel lay before them, a sparkling, emerald green. Over that glassine sea of green, a china-blue sky vast as eternity. It was such a crystal-clear day that Fargo could easily see the Channel Islands.

"Dear heart of God!" Lindy exclaimed upon her first view of an ocean. "So this is the mighty Pacific? It goes on forever!"

"It's no pee puddle," Fargo agreed. "Prob'ly take a feller most of one day to swim across it."

Despite his joke, Fargo, too, was visibly impressed. He

had seen oceans before, and it always amazed him how similar they looked to the rolling green plains of the nation's interior.

"Fargo!" Rick Cully shouted. "Damn it, man, we're eatin' dust back here. Why'n'cha let us take turns riding in the wagon?"

"I'd rather buy ready-to-wear boots," Fargo retorted.

He kneed the Ovaro into motion again. The softer trail was doing wonders for the stallion's hooves. He slackened the reins and gave the Ovaro his head at first, letting him snuff the ground good. A horse in unfamiliar country settled down quickly once it got the smell of the place.

Newt clucked to the team, and the wagon lurched into motion. The trail was wide enough to ride beside Fargo.

"So we're finally bound for San Francisco," Lindy said, flashing those dazzling teeth at Fargo in a grateful smile.

"I told you I'd find a good man, didn't I? Well, here I am."

Lindy lowered her voice. "Oh, you're good, all right. I can't stop thinking *how* good. Takes my breath away."

"Can't hang a woman for her thoughts," he reminded her.

"Or a man, right?"

Fargo grinned. "Right, or I'd've died a million times."

Lindy turned serious. "I am sorry about your job, Skye. But as you said, we're paying more."

Earlier Fargo had stopped at the Pacific & Western Railroad field office in Santa Paula. His new employers were eager for his services and not too thrilled at this delay. Still, they granted him a few extra weeks.

"If law and order are ever established out here," Newt said, still gazing left toward the beautiful vista of the sea, "it's going to be a paradise."

Fargo nodded. "I figure I've seen just about every nook and cranny of the West. You'd have to go into the Yellowstone country or the Teton range to match the raw beauty. But 'raw' is the word."

" 'At's right, Fargo," Cully goaded. *"Raw."*

"Raw works both ways, muttonhead," Fargo reminded him. "Look down at your clothing. The lice are drowning."

Cully didn't look. He'd been next in line behind Robles and now wore much of the man's blood.

An hour passed without incident although Fargo remained constantly vigilant—this trail might be easy going for the horses, but this was also bandit-infested country. Even here, with an ocean protecting one entire flank, Fargo wished he had a point rider to send out, along with a flanker up in the steep slopes on their right.

"We're bumping shoulders with mountains!" a delighted Lindy exclaimed.

She meant the Coast Ranges, pressing in from their right flank—sometimes crowding almost to the lip of the Pacific before falling off in sheer cliffs.

"They're pretty, all right," Fargo conceded. "But they'll give us trouble before this trip is over."

"Trouble? How?"

"There's one kind of trouble right there," Fargo replied, nodding ahead. Several huge boulders—one the size of a covered wagon—blocked the trail.

"We can squeeze around or through 'em," Newt said.

"Sure we can. But rock slides are more common in upper California, and there's a damn good chance we'll get caught in one while it's happening."

Fargo pointed to another low rock heap beside the trail. "That's the fifth one I've counted since we left Los Angeles. They're called traveler's graves. The rocks are heaped on the dead to keep animals off—but some of those same rocks did the killing."

He pointed up the slopes. "It ain't just rocks. This time of year there's sudden, heavy rains on the coast, and flash floods with mud slides are a constant danger. Entire caravans have been washed into the sea in an eyeblink."

Fargo nudged the Ovaro across the trail to a stand of sycamore and weeping birch. Using his Henry, he pointed to a spot where one of the trees had been clawed high up.

"Another thing—either of you got any idea what this is?"

Both greenhorns shook their heads.

"That's where a silvertip bear—a grizzly, some call it—has marked this territory as his. These mountains are crawling with them. The grizz is the worst animal threat on any trail, especially when charging. Few rifles can bring one down in time."

Lindy cast a nervous glance at how deep those claw

marks were—and how high. "They don't stay up in the mountains?"

"Their dens are way up there, sure," Fargo said. "But any foraging bear will travel miles, especially toward the smell of water. That's why we're keeping that Sharps loaded—it's the only weapon we have that *might* drop one."

"Sounds to me," Lindy complained, "like you're trying to scare us."

"Not scare, darlin'. Just educate you to the dangers."

Fargo was bothered by the way Newt and Lindy were acting since gaining the trail. Like too many naive tenderfeet buried in those shallow graves, they were being lulled by scenic beauty, warm sunshine, the twittering of birds and the dusty twang of grasshoppers' wings. But California was *not* Fiddler's Green—was in fact some of the most violent ground in America.

"Any chance," Fargo remarked casually, "that Wagner whoever he is, will have more surprises waiting for us?"

Lindy flushed, Newt averted his gaze, and Fargo gave a harsh bark of laughter.

"At least I know you two are decent," Fargo said. "You can't lie worth a shit."

Fargo let it go. After all, Lindy said she was sworn to silence. Fargo, like any frontiersman worth his buckskins, believed that a man's word was his bond. He despised a liar as did the Indians, and he wouldn't ask Lindy to break her oath.

He also realized he was in deep trouble. Those cold-blooded killers behind the wagon had peers galore. Even if Fargo survived the trail, he would be entering lawless San Francisco with a woman who was obviously at the heart of something dangerous.

"Pile on the agony," he muttered to his stallion, squaring his shoulders for whatever was coming.

8

The first day along the Old Mission Trail was uneventful with the exception of a few Klamath Indians begging for food. Fargo's group spent the night camped in a sheltered cove, moonlight dancing on the waves.

The three surviving prisoners were talking among themselves in low tones and sending Fargo plenty of hooded glances.

"Keep a close eye on those buzzards, Newt," Fargo muttered over morning coffee. "I could tell they wanted to avoid Los Angeles. But the idea of going to San Francisco scares them even more. They're laying plans."

They set out early, Fargo hoping to make good time. Point Conception, one hundred twenty miles out from Los Angeles, was the first major landmark, and Fargo expected to reach it day after tomorrow.

"Panther piss?" Newt inquired, proffering the bottle of bourbon.

Fargo grinned. Newt had not called it "whiskey" yet. He was showing what an old frontier salt he had become.

"Too early for me," Fargo declined.

"Not for us, crusader," Cully called out. "We're dry as a year-old cow chip. Sail that bottle back here, why'n'cha?"

"Don't start with the mouth, Cully," Fargo warned calmly. "I got damn little patience left for it."

"Yeah? You'll take it and you'll *like* it, you sanctimonious bastard."

"We'll just see about that," Fargo promised.

Both Lindy and Newt, Fargo noticed, were showing signs of travel strain. By necessity, Fargo had the endurance of a doorknob. However, his two companions, while plucky, were not used to the rigors of what amounted to a forced march.

Nonetheless, Lindy was clearly enthralled by this beautiful vista of bottomless blue sky, endless green ocean, and dramatic shoreline of steep cliffs and gigantic boulders.

"Oh, Skye, isn't it just gorgeous?" she enthused.

Skye nodded. Without question this beautiful, lush country was vastly different from the Southwest terrain he recently traversed to get here—that desolate country of juniper and sage, of deep arroyos and steep mesas. However, he wasn't lulled by California's beauty and apparent peacefulness—at any moment it could erupt in deadly violence, for this was still a lawless land.

Lindy, pretty in a blue gingham dress and starched white bonnet, read some of Fargo's misgivings in his face.

"Why such a Gloomy Gus?" she teased him. "Since we escaped from Los Angeles, the trip's been like a Sunday carriage ride in the park. Those poor Indians we fed yesterday were actually nice."

Fargo agreed, but he never relaxed in Indian country. Fortunately, the situation out here, with the scores of California tribes, was nothing like Texas, where Comanches on the scrap had wiped out entire settlements along the Rio Grande. Or in the Arizona Territory, where even now whites and Apaches waged mutual wars of extermination.

"It's not the Indians we need to fret most," Fargo told her. "There's dozens of organized road gangs up and down this coast."

Lindy, her face puzzled, pointed toward the mountains pressing in on their right.

"I don't understand it," she said. "Why so many gangs? I thought fortunes in gold were being pulled out of those mountains?"

"Actually," Fargo corrected the greenhorn, grinning, "that's the Coast Range you're pointing at. The gold is in the Sierras behind them. There *were* plenty of fortunes being made, all right, though the 'rush' is a slow trickle now. Especially with the Comstock Lode east of here luring miners."

"Besides, sis," Newt tossed in, "I've read in *Harper's* how there haven't been *that* many fortunes made. With the grossly inflated prices in a gold camp, a man can go broke before he even gets directions to his diggings. So then he gets hungry, he gets mad, he joins a gang. If—*Jesus!*"

Newt drew rein so quickly that the prisoners tripped over each other. Fargo saw the flash of grizzled, yellow-brown fur at the same time Newt did—a full-grown female grizzly lumbering across the trail ahead of them. Two small cubs trailed her.

"Newt," Fargo said quietly, struggling to calm his nervous Ovaro, "hand me that Sharps."

"You're going to *shoot* them?" Lindy protested.

"Only the mother *if* I have to," Fargo assured her, placing a priming cap on the big rifle's nipple. "A she-grizz with cubs is highly protective of her young. She hasn't seen us, and she's upwind of our scent, so we'll just sit quiet. Their den's up high in the mountains, but they've headed down to the water to look for fish."

"Oh, Christsakes, the great white hunter!" Cully mocked. " 'Fraid of a damn grizz! I could kill that mucking bear with just a good knife—done it plenty. Tell me, Fargo— how are you able to diddle that pretty piece of tail sittin' beside you? Hell, it's obvious you ain't even got a pizzle 'tween your legs."

All three prisoners shook with mirth, even the taciturn Stone Lofley.

"Brash as a government mule, ain't you, Cully?" Fargo remarked, swinging down from the saddle and handing the big Sharps to Newt. "You just made your brag how you're a mighty killer of grizzly bears. Now you can make good on it."

Fargo pulled the Arkansas toothpick from its boot sheath, then drew his Colt to cover Cully. "Newt, untie him from the leadline. Cully, I *pray* you try a fox play on me— I'll blow your skull apart like a piñata."

"The hell you doing?" the tall, beanpole thin hardcase demanded nervously.

"Giving you a chance to show us what a mighty killer you are," Fargo said, leading Cully toward the sea and a steep slope, down which the bears had gone to reach the rock-strewn shoreline.

"Hey! Hey, Fargo, has your brain gone soft?" Cully whined. "You can't do this!"

Fargo untied the prisoner's hands. "I can't, huh? You've insulted me, the lady, and her brother repeatedly. I gave you several warnings, but you just love to flap your gums, don't you, owlhoot? You've bragged about killing several grizz bears with a knife. So I'll tell you what—go kill *her.*"

Fargo slapped his knife in Cully's hand, then centered a boot in his back and gave a mighty push. Cully went catapulting down the slope, so terrified he gave a high-pitched scream as he bounced along.

By the time Cully finished tumbling, the she-grizz had spotted him. The terrified criminal sat motionless at the base of the slope. The grizzly, unable to trust the weak eyesight of her species, rose up high on her hind legs to sample the air with her nose.

When she caught the man scent, she loosed a deep, bellowing roar of rage and hatred. The unnerving sound made the fine hairs on Fargo's arms stiffen.

"Fargo!" Cully begged, his voice squeaky with fright. "Fargo, *shoot* the son of a bitch, wouldja? The joke's gone far enough, I—Oh, *Christ!*"

Cully lost the power of speech as the mammoth animal charged across the beach toward him. The curved claws, Fargo estimated, were a foot long, and one swipe would shred a man to rag tatters. The dripping yellow fangs were perhaps half that length—the most lethal killing machine in the West.

"Fargo!" Cully shrieked as the grizzled mountain monster thundered closer, determined to protect her young. "Have mercy, man! Shoot that big she-bitch!"

"Mercy," Fargo muttered. As if Cully or his filthy ilk ever showed mercy to any of their victims.

"Are you going to let the bear kill him, Skye?" Lindy's voice asked behind him. The bear had slowed her charge to advance more cautiously.

"Not exactly. I'm going to shoot one bullet *near* the bear. I refuse to kill her to save Cully—he's not worth orphaning those cubs. If that one shot spooks the grizz, fine. If not, Cully is no longer our problem."

"To hell with that murderer," Newt put in, handing the Sharps back to Fargo. "You don't owe him a chance."

"Yes, he does," Lindy gainsaid. "Skye is a better man

than those prisoners; he can't sink to their level. He's the Trailsman, and that has to mean something."

"Fargo!" Cully shrieked, for now the grizzly was only fifteen feet away, woofing aggressively and giving the terrified thug an impressive view of those claws and fangs. "Fargo, this ain't right! It's outright murder!"

"Hell, Cully, ain't you got a pizzle 'tween your legs?" Fargo taunted, using Cully's own words. "*You* can kill that mucking bear with just a good knife, remember? Well, you *got* a good knife, so skin that grizz while I send the next one down!"

But Cully had lost any vestige of manhood he ever owned. As the grizzly moved in so close that her shadow enveloped the cowering man, Cully let out a scream of terror so high-pitched it sounded feminine. He dropped the Arkansas toothpick in the sand, covered his face with his hands, and rolled into a tight ball.

"Hell," said a disappointed Fargo, tossing the big Sharps into his shoulder socket and thumbing back the hammer. "Like the lady said, I'm the Trailsman."

The fifteen-pound gun rocked Fargo back on his heels when the slug, propelled by seven hundred grains of black powder, rocketed from the muzzle. The explosive roar of detonation echoed down the rocky beach, momentarily dwarfing the surf noise. A powerful geyser of sand flew up at the grizzly's feet, and moments later she and her cubs fled to the north.

"Get your skinny ass up here, Cully!" Fargo snapped to the cowering, whimpering man. "And bring my knife—unless it's still in the bear," he added sarcastically.

For Lindy's sake Fargo tried not to laugh when Cully, so humiliated he couldn't lift his gaze from his feet, topped the slope—the front of his sailcloth trousers sopping wet. His ruthless companions, however, were less delicate.

"Cully, you *pissed* yourself!" Coyote mocked him. "You weak sister!"

Even Stone Lofley's broad, blunt face, usually expressionless as a sanded board, was split by a scornful smile. Just then Fargo realized something interesting: It wasn't all three hardcases Lindy refused to look at—just Lofley. Right now he, too, was definitely refusing to look at her. Nor was

Lindy the kind of woman *any* man, especially in the woman-starved West, would avoid looking at.

Unless he was hoping not to be recognized.

"Just curious," Fargo said quietly to Lindy when the party was again in motion. "Have you and Stone Lofley encountered each other somewhere before?"

Lindy looked straight at him. "I'm done lying to you, Skye. Yes, we've encountered each other. That's all I can possibly tell you."

Fargo sighed, then nodded. "I'm glad you told me that much. Because now I know there'll be more coming to kill you. Somebody wants you dead, and wants it bad. Looks like I'm gonna *earn* that ten dollars a day."

The Old Mission Trail was better in some places than in others. Fargo's party might make five or ten miles without major difficulties, only to reach a washout or a jumble of boulders.

"Whoa!" Fargo called out toward the end of the afternoon.

"What's wrong?" Newt asked, drawing back on the reins.

A few miles back they had gone through an expanse of mud as thick and sloppy as gumbo, caused by a nearby creek running over its banks. Fargo pointed at the mud-caked tires of the wagon.

"That'll wear any team out quicker 'n scat. We'll need to scrape 'em."

Fargo employed his Arkansas toothpick, Newt a curved skinning knife that Fargo carried in a saddlebag, and the iron tires were quickly skimmed clean.

Cully wasn't mouthing off since the incident with the grizzly. Fargo realized, however, that he definitely had not been humbled—only enraged. Now he watched Fargo from malevolent eyes like burning pools of acid, hate mallet-stamped into his features.

"You can stare at me until the sun sets in the east," Fargo's mild voice told the murdering coward. "But the truth is this—if I untie you right now and give you the chance to fight me fair and square—guns *or* knuckles—you won't do it. That's because you're a murderer, not a fighter."

Cully averted his eyes, muttering something Fargo didn't catch.

"Hey? That offer go for me and Stone, too, Fargo?" Coyote asked.

"All right, we'll start with you. Guns or knuckles?" Fargo asked, reaching for the Apache's ropes.

"Ahh . . . just roweling you," Coyote said with a burst of nervous laughter. "Leave them ropes be. Hell, I *like* you, Fargo. I'd let you top my sister."

"I feel so damned honored," Fargo said dryly, swinging up into leather again and kneeing the Ovaro forward.

That muddy expanse, a few miles back, had Fargo thinking. At this time of the year the California coast was vulnerable to sudden downpours. With mountains crowding them on one side, unstable landslide slopes worried him. One good rain could turn this trail into a hog wallow, delaying them for days. That could be disastrous because by now Fargo was convinced that whatever appointment Lindy had to keep was indeed important.

Unable to scout ahead, yet realizing more attacks against Lindy were likely, Fargo kept a constant eye to the heavily wooded mountain slopes on their right. He also watched the trail below him closely.

"Skye, why do you keep doing that?" Lindy complained petulantly. "We lose time whenever you do it."

She was right—each time Fargo spotted hoofprints along the trail, he swung down to crouch over them with studious concentration.

"It ain't losing time when you're being careful," he replied. "See how the grass is flattened inside the prints? That tells me how recently they were made. If it's still flat, that's recent. It it's sprung back up, it's old. These are old."

They were not alone on the trail. California, like all of the West, was rife with various itinerant workers, ranging from rat catchers to circuit judges. Fargo carefully checked each one they passed, his palm on the butt of his Colt.

Now and then a grinding squeal rose from the back of the wagon.

"Newt!" Fargo called out each time, reining in. "Bucket duty, old son."

Lindy frowning at every delay, Newt would scramble

down and slither under the wagon. The axles had to be continually greased from a bucket that swung underneath the wagon.

Toward sundown they reached a long-abandoned log-hut fort, much of it burned for firewood. Fargo glanced around.

"Well, there's good wind shelter and fresh water. Not much graze, but we've got plenty of oats for the horses. Let's camp here."

Fargo, covering the prisoners with his Henry, led them into some tall bushes to answer the call of nature. Then he settled each prisoner against his own tree, tying him securely. He kept them widely separated so they couldn't easily plan together.

While Lindy washed some beans for supper, Fargo and Newt unhitched the wagon team, freeing the tug chains from the singletrees and unbuckling the harness.

"Use deadwood for the fire," Fargo advised Lindy when he spotted her gathering green sticks. "It doesn't smoke."

"You listen to the big crusader, cupcake," Coyote jeered. "That's the first thing us big, bad outlaws on the dodge learn."

Lindy got a pot of beans cooking while Fargo stripped the leather from his Ovaro. He put the stallion on a long ground-tether, then fed him oats from his hat. He glanced with guilt at the black-and-white pinto's ratty mane and the burrs marring his coat. Usually he tried to curry the stallion morning and night. But having a string of ruthless killers to feed, water, and generally nursemaid cut into a man's free time.

"Skye?" Newt asked, walking up beside him after feeding the team horses. "One thing I don't get. Ever since we left Los Angeles, there's been telegraph poles alongside the trail—and the wire is intact, I can hear it humming."

"So? The telegraph is all over the country now. This is a state, after all."

"Yeah, sure. What I mean is, between road gangs and Indians, wouldn't you think it would be constantly cut? Things would go a lot worse for travelers like us that way."

"Maybe," Fargo said. "But in territory this vast, the road gangs depend on the telegraph too. They need it to keep each other informed of potential victims and to send warnings about posses. One Indian could easily bring down the telegraph. But most of them are scared spitless by the talking wire and won't touch it. Heap big medicine."

By now a huge, bloodred sun had almost slipped into the ocean. An uneasy premonition licked at Fargo's belly, and he took a long walk around their campsite, making sure they were alone. By the time he returned to camp, an ascending moon lighted the very tips of the coast mountains like silver patina.

Bad trouble coming, Fargo, he told himself. *The worst. This girl has got somebody scared bad, and more killers are coming.*

"Soup's on, Skye," Lindy greeted him. "Though it's hardly soup—just boiled beans with salt and pepper."

They dipped hardtack into the beans. The large wafers of unleavened bread were tasteless, but quickly filling. Fargo kept glancing toward the shadows beyond the sawing flames of the campfire—he thought he heard Rick Cully and Coyote talking to each other. Stone Lofley appeared to have dozed off, but Fargo suspected it was the quiet ones who missed nothing.

"No offense, sis," Newt complained, tossing out some of his beans. "This tastes like boiled shoes. *All* the food out west tastes like bilge."

"Bless God for a good stomach," Fargo agreed cheerfully, eating with gusto. Bad digestion, and the wretched food that caused it, had ruined the dreams of countless prospectors, trappers and others. Fargo had a cast-iron stomach. "Any more?" he added, handing his bowl to Lindy.

"I don't mind the poor quality of the food so much," Lindy said, ladling out more beans for Fargo. "But these prices out here, for everything, are positively criminal. Back home you can get a bushel of potatoes for twenty-five cents, a bushel of oats for thirty cents. Out here, a *can* of peas is three dollars!"

"It ain't criminal," Fargo corrected her. "It's what gold does. It's no different on the Comstock or out in Pikes Peak country. A man can bake a few trays of bear sign or biscuits and make a year's wages in one day selling to hungry prospectors."

An owl hooted nearby, and Fargo's premonition of danger was back. First he checked all the prisoners' ropes; then he again made a slow ambit of their campsite. Nothing seemed amiss, but when he glanced down toward the dark beach and moonlit ocean he felt his scalp tighten. It seemed highly unlikely, though, that paid killers or anyone else would pick this wild stretch of coastline to hide in ambush. The mountain slopes to the right of the trail offered much better vantage.

When he returned to camp, Lindy and Newt were hotly arguing.

"Jesus," Fargo cut in, laughing, "are you two married? Come down off your hind legs, both of you. The hell you scrapping about?"

Newt pointed straight up at the starry sky. "I just read an article in *Scientific American* that claims there's more stars in the sky than grains of sand on all the world's beaches."

"Impossible," Lindy snapped.

Fargo yawned, watching the shadowy forms of the prisoners. "Has anybody bothered to count either one?"

Newt laughed as if Fargo were a child. "Of course not. It can't be done. That's why we have to trust the experts."

"Wasn't all that long ago," Fargo said, "when these scientist fellows were swearing on a stack of Bibles that birds from Earth winter on the moon. *I* wouldn't buy a horse from 'em, Newt."

"Think I'll count some stars myself," Lindy said, her eyes meeting Fargo's in the flickering firelight. "Is the ocean safe to bathe in?"

"Don't go out too far," he warned, "or the undertow could surprise you. There's a chill in the air, but you'll find the water still warm from summer."

"I'd feel safer with a guard," Lindy said, fighting back a smile at her own naughtiness.

"Better safe than sorry," Fargo agreed, palming the wheel of his Colt and giving it a puff to clear the blow sand out. "Newt, take this and keep it with you. Any of those prisoners makes a play, drill him."

Fargo picked up his Henry and levered a round into the chamber. Lindy took lye soap, a towel, and clean clothing from a valise in the wagon. They debouched from the wooded area around the old fort and crossed the rocky beach, forced to raise their voices above the sound of roaring surf.

Fargo paused, glancing all around.

"Something wrong?" Lindy asked.

"Prob'ly not," Fargo admitted. "I've had a feeling since we stopped to camp, is all. All these big boulders make good ambush points."

Lindy's laughter was musical, a silvery tinkle. "Ambush? Skye, aren't you taking your job *too* seriously? Who would ambush us out here, and at night? Maybe this will help relax you."

They were close to the furling waves now, out of sight of those back in camp. Lindy boldly unbuttoned her dress and peeled it off, letting the wind take it until it fluttered to the ground. Fargo felt a flush of loin heat at the way her nipples dinted the linen fabric of her chemise.

She shucked off the chemise, then her frilly pantaloons, standing before him naked as a newborn in the creamy moonlight.

"You need a bath, too, big fellow," she called over her shoulder as she raced out into the ocean. "C'mon!"

Fargo watched that pretty little strawberries 'n' cream ass, firm and high-split, bouncing merrily out to sea. He wrenched off his boots, peeled off his buckskins, laid the Henry on his clothing.

Fargo started toward the water, then froze in place. For a moment he thought he'd heard boot leather scrape a rock behind him.

"Skye!" Lindy's delighted voice tempted him. "C'mon! The water's great! There's something I'd like to . . . try with you!"

All around Fargo, huge, oddly shaped boulders loomed, their shadows sinister; but Lindy's last, suggestive remark had turned his shaft hard as sacked salt.

"Oh, my, *yes!*" she greeted him in water up to her thighs. She wrapped a hand around his curved saber and stroked it slowly, sending hot, tickling waves of pleasure through it. "So big and *so* nice," she cooed, dropping down onto her knees. "I know I'm being wanton, Skye, but I *have* to taste it."

"I'm not one to discourage a woman's impulses," Fargo

assured her. He added a happy sigh as moist, tight heat flowed over his shaft when she took it into her hungry mouth.

Fargo reached down to take a firm, impressive breast in each hand. Lindy sucked and nibbled as much of him as she could, pumping the rest of his length in a tight fist that made Fargo moan encouragement. While she treated him, he returned the favor by tweaking her nipples until they were hard and pointy.

Pleasure built to a hot, tight pressure in Fargo's groin. Lindy, feeling him turn steel hard, knew what was coming. She doubled her exertions, keening in her excitement, and Fargo's entire body twitched out of control when he spent himself.

Fargo, too, folded to his knees, left weak by his release.

"Let's go spread my towel on the beach," Lindy urged, tugging him toward shore with her.

"Slow down, girl!" Fargo pleaded with a grin. "Even a studhorse needs a few minutes to—*unh*!"

Fargo staggered hard left, almost falling. His harsh grunt of pain was caused by a fist-sized rock smashing into his right elbow. The arm immediately turned hot and went numb, feeling useless to Fargo. He ducked just in time to avoid a second rock headed straight for his head.

Lindy let out a piercing scream as a huge, shadowy figure lunged at Fargo, a long spear thrust out before him!

9

For a breathless moment, as the attacker rushed him like a wolverine unleashed, Fargo feared this was the end of his last trail. Trying to stop that long spear seemed more dangerous than avoiding it, so he launched himself toward shore in a diving somersault, the spear missing him by a cat whisker.

The attacker immediately spun around to pursue him.

"Watch out, Skye!" Lindy cried out. "He's right behind you!"

I can't *die bare-ass naked,* Fargo told himself as he made a mad dash toward his Henry. Evidently the attacker hadn't seen it, or he wouldn't have to resort to rocks and spears.

The Henry was still there, all right. So was the dogged attacker—Fargo could hear his feet pounding through the surf, his raspy breathing. Only when Fargo reached out with his right arm to grab the weapon, however, did he realize the trouble he was in.

He had wisely charged the Henry earlier, but his arm, still numb from that rock to his elbow, was all but useless to him. Fargo could grip the rifle's trigger mechanism, but not lift the Henry. Nor was there time, with his mystery assailant within spitting distance, to switch to his clumsier, slower left arm. He had perhaps one second to save his own life.

Once again his vast experience saved Fargo. Several years ago he had joined a party scouting through the Wasatch Range of Utah Territory. When Ute Indians stole all their provisions, the men came to the brink of starvation and grew so weak they couldn't even lift their heavy rifles to shoot game. One old trapper invented something he called the "swinging snapshot," and Fargo relied on it now to save his bacon.

He didn't waste time trying to lift the rifle. Instead, he gripped it hard as he could and then swung his entire body around hard and fast, pulling the rifle with him. Momentum, not muscle, brought the Henry's muzzle up just briefly; timing it perfectly, Fargo fired at the figure rushing him.

A sharp, surprised grunt, a skidding of feet, and the attacker flopped to the beach, feet jerking a few times until his nervous system caught up with the fact of death.

"Skye!" Lindy cried out hysterically. "Are you . . . Is he . . . ?"

"He's dead," Fargo confirmed, kneeling beside the body and feeling for a neck pulse. "I'm not."

"Skye! Lindy!" Newt's worried voice bellowed from camp. "You two all right?"

"No problems here," Fargo called back. "Just keep a close eye on those prisoners."

Shivering now in the blustery night wind, Fargo and Lindy hurriedly dressed.

"Another hired killer?" Lindy asked, looking at the body in the ghostly blue moonlight. Her voice was almost lost in the roar of the ocean.

Fargo shook his head. He had been forced to kill in self-defense, but wished he could somehow take this bullet back.

"Not a hired killer," he said. "A paid jobber would have firearms and pick a better spot. He wouldn't be so clumsy at killing, either. This is just a bracero."

"A who?"

"A poor Mexican worker. They come up here by the thousands to pan gold and work for the mining companies, any work they can get. He's been out of work a long time, by the look of his boots and his barrel-stave ribs. I'd say he lives along this beach because the tide sometimes brings in dead fish and other stuff he can use."

"But . . . then why did he attack you? We'd have given him food if he visited our camp."

"*We* would, sure, but in California there's strong feeling against Mexicans since the days of the Bear Flag Revolt.

They're sometimes shot on sight, and a few deserve it. This one decided to turn killer, and it cost him."

"You had no choice, Skye."

He nodded. "The way you say. It was his decision and I got no regrets. Still, there's no bragging rights in killing a fellow who's down on his luck."

Lindy carefully looked at Fargo's elbow. "It's going to bruise awfully, but there's little broken skin or blood. Hurt?"

"Like the dickens," he admitted. "That jasper's got—uh, *had*—a throwing arm like Newt's. But the numbness is clearing up and I'm getting strength back in it."

He wrapped his good left arm around Lindy, carried the Henry in his right. "Let's get back to camp, lady. Newt's all alone with those hardcases—and who knows how many more uninvited guests will show up before morning."

In two days and nights of hard travel on fast horses, Terrible Jack Slade and his favorite lackey, Lumpy Neck McGuire, made good time heading south from San Francisco. Now they commanded an excellent ambush position north of Point Conception and just south of La Purisima Mission.

"We made the trip in jig time, Lumpy," Slade gloated as they began to strip the tack from their exhausted and sore-used mounts. "They haven't passed this spot yet, or we'd've met 'em on the road."

Lumpy Neck was a former member of the Hounds, the first vigilantes in San Francisco. He was named for the huge goiter distorting his neck. His tie-down holsters held two Colt Navy sidearms tucked in butt-first. For close-in killing he packed a double-ten express gun—a sawed-off ten-gauge shotgun, favored by stagecoach guards.

"We'll be shooting fish in a barrel," he predicted smugly. "Hell, it's too easy, Jack. Let's wear blinders to keep it sporting."

Slade shook his head violently, staring down the moonlit slope to the trail below. Unlike run-of-the-mill vigilantes, who were usually found in saloons telling whoppers about their supposed exploits, Slade had vast experience from his days as a war spy in Mexico. He had chosen Lumpy Neck for this job because he had spent fifteen years living wit the Sioux in the Platte Valley, learning the art of bruta killing and stealth. Nonetheless, Slade believed *no one* wa qualified to face Skye Fargo except maybe all the devil in hell.

"Push that fish-in-a-barrel crap from your thoughts righ now," he said sternly. "This damn Trailsman is a nerv cuss, and he *won't* give up the ghost easy. One little mi take, and me 'n' you're gone-up cases."

Slade wore a long gray duster to protect his clothing an firearms. His beloved whip protruded from his belt.

"Christsakes, look at your horse," Lumpy Neck said staring at the seventeen-hand blood bay Slade rode. "So of a bitch is really puffin' and blowin'."

Slade's horse was indeed breathing hard from the grue ing pace its master had set. Even in the stingy moonligh it was easy to see dried blood smearing the bay's shoulder To Slade, a horse was just a tool like any other, replaceabl when it broke. Before he left San Francisco, he had file down his spurs to gouge more speed from his mount.

"Never mind my damn horse," Slade said. "We're her to get some killing done. Look here."

Slade took a neatly folded bandanna from his shi pocket and carefully opened it up. Lumpy Neck stared the four strange objects now revealed—.44 shells, hollowe out at the tip where a .22 blank had been inserted in eac

"*Hell,* yeah, your explosive bullets," he finally said. " 'member when you used one a them on that big, harel Swede who wouldn't sell Wagner his diggin's. Shit, it pla tered the whole front of his head all over a tree."

"Damn straight," Slade boasted, hefting his Hunt r peating rifle. "I used Patsy Plumb here to do it, too. It be an even closer shot from here."

"Fargo first, hey?"

Slade shook his head. "Wagner talks like a damn bool but he's right—from here on out, everybody else is sma potatoes compared to the woman. Until she's dead, nor of us who draw wages from Wagner can rest easy."

"Yeah, but . . . Skye Fargo, small potatoes? That's lik calling Texas a corner lot."

Slade gave his subordinate a pitying look. "Lumpy,

least pretend you got more brains than a rabbit. Of course we have to kill Fargo, and mighty damn quick. A crusader like him won't abide the killing of a woman, especially not one he's escorting. But Fargo ain't sittin' on information that could put us in prison or get us hanged—that damn bitch is. Besides . . ."

Slade pulled Judge Lash from his belt, missing the feel of the rough leather whip in his hand.

"I want Fargo's head on display in a pickling jar," he announced bluntly. "I been studying on the idea. Fargo's a true-blue, blown-in-the-bottle crusader. He's made plenty of enemies in his travels, and men will line up all day long to pay four bits and see Fargo's head in brine."

"Fetch more money than a tiger in a cage," Lumpy Neck agreed.

"But first," Slade went on, stroking Judge Lash, "we need to capture that crusading meddler alive. I'm going to tie him to a tree and give him a taste of the cowhide—brother, I mean whip him till his hair falls out."

Lumpy Neck was tough as bore bristles, but didn't like the sound of this plan—or the sound of Slade's tone. It made him edgy. Terrible Jack had caught the war sickness down in Mexico, and now killing a man was easier for him than rolling off a log. Lumpy Neck had once seen him kill an old man just for snoring. However, killing, by itself, no longer satisfied Slade—there had to be horrific suffering first or he felt cheated.

"A dangerous man like Fargo," Lumpy Neck suggested tactfully, "ought to be killed quick. Same way you'd kill a charging bobcat."

Slade nodded toward Lumpy Neck's sawed-off shotgun. "Nerve up. Once we capture Fargo, at the first sign of trouble you can fill his belly full of Blue Whistlers. But *don't* mess up his head, you hear?"

Lumpy Neck grabbed for a small oilcloth satchel Slade had tied to Lumpy's rented sorrel before they rode out from San Francisco.

"Katy Christ!" Slade swore, staying his hand. "Easy with that, boy."

He opened it up to show Lumpy Neck the dynamite and cans of blasting powder within.

"*That's* why you tied that bag to my horse," Lumpy Neck fumed. "So it would be me who got blowed sky-high if those explosives got shook too hard."

Slade's face divided in a rare grin. "Ain't life a bitch? You made it in one piece, so quit pissing and moaning. This high-power stuff is our ace in the hole in case my explosive bullets don't work."

"Hell, why not just start right off with it, Jack? Ain't no need to even aim them big-talking sticks."

"Nah, we'll hold off a bit, anyway," Slade insisted. "No need to kill Cully and them if we can help it. Nor to let Fargo off the hook by killing him instantly."

"Just so you can flog him and collect his head?" Lumpy Neck said. "Christ, let's just blow 'em all to hell and make this easy."

"*I'm* the he-bear right now, Lumpy. Besides, it ain't just my wantin' to cage Fargo before we kill him. Use your think piece. If we toss dynamite along this trail, that points right back to San Francisco, only place it's sold in the state. This Helzer woman's comin' out here to accuse Wagner and everybody knows Wagner sells explosives to the mining companies. It's a risky clue."

Slade fell silent and watched how false dawn had begun to lighten the eastern sky.

"Sunrise soon," he said. "I don't know exactly where Fargo and the rest are. But it's strong odds they'll pass this spot sometime this morning. Let's grab forty winks, then get into position."

Moving gingerly, favoring his sore right elbow, Fargo rolled up his blanket and groundsheet and secured them under the cantle straps of his saddle. The sun was well up but had not yet broken over the Coast Range. The Pacific rolled in gentle swells and looked almost black without sunshine reflecting off it.

"Jesus Christ, Fargo," Cully snapped. "Comb the pussy hair out of your teeth and get this medicine show on the road, wouldja? I gotta piss like a racehorse."

"At least I've *got* teeth," Fargo warned him. "Don't start with me, Cully."

One by one he untied each man and led him into the bushes, a cocked Colt on them the entire time. Cully had learned his lesson yesterday, when Fargo tossed him to the bears, and didn't even give him a dirty look. However, Coyote's eyes shifted to all sides while he made water, and the Apache seemed on the brink of some reckless move.

"It's your life, old son," Fargo remarked quietly. He wagged the barrel of his Colt for emphasis, wincing at the jolt of pain in his elbow. "You want to get it over quick, that's your choice."

Coyote laughed and made a surrendering gesture, raising both hands. "Maybe so, better not, uh? Fargo, you *are* bad medicine. Sure you ain't Apache?"

It was Stone Lofley, though, who truly gave Fargo the fantods as he led the big bull of a man off into the bushes. As usual the hardcase was silent and brooding, his broad, blunt face offering no clues to his thoughts or emotions—not that Fargo was sure he had any.

"Do you ever talk, Lofley?" Fargo asked. "Or have Indians cut out your tongue?"

"I talk," Lofley replied while easing his bladder, "when I want to. Not when I'm told to."

"Fair enough. You want to talk about Lindy Helzer?"

"If that's a female name, I don't know the bitch."

"Hell, you don't," Fargo gainsaid. "She's the woman traveling with us. The one Wagner sent you knuckleheads to kill."

A grin twitched Lofley's cracked lips apart. "Her? When do I get a turn at poking her? You're hoggin' all of it."

Fargo shook his head, not fooled by the thug's feigned ignorance. "You know her, and she knows you. But both of you are working mighty hard at pretending otherwise. Why?"

Lofley closed his fly. "Damn, Fargo, you been smokin' the Chinese pipe? How would a high-toned, quality bitch like her know a hard-living jasper like me?"

"Good question, but she knows you. It's got to do with her dead sister, right?"

"Piss off, crusader," Lofley snapped, his horse trader's eyes fleeing from Fargo's steady, lake blue stare. "When do we eat? I'm so hungry my backbone's rubbin' 'gainst my ribs."

Fargo covered all three prisoners while they ate a simple meal of dried fruit and hardtack. When the captives were tied to the lead line again, ready for travel, Fargo joined Lindy and Newt for his own quick breakfast. They ate the same Spartan fare as the prisoners, with the addition of black coffee strong enough to float a horseshoe.

"I see you're favoring your elbow," Lindy remarked to the Trailsman. "I have laudanum."

Fargo shook his head and pointed toward the prisoners with his tin coffee cup. "Thanks, but this is no time or place to be feeling groggy."

"Maybe a jolt of who-shot-John?" Newt offered the bottle of bourbon, but Fargo waved it off.

"We're making good progress?" Lindy asked.

"Not too bad," Fargo said. "We should reach Point Conception by forenoon."

He paused and glanced over his shoulder toward the steep slope bordering the east side of the Old Mission Trail. It was teeming with blue columbine and sweet clover, with the lacy white flower known as Queen Anne's Lace.

"That's assuming," he added, "that we don't have any unpleasant surprises. I wouldn't bet much, though, on that assumption. I'm also worried about the weather."

Lindy had been avoiding his eyes. At this remark, however, she met his gaze and burst out laughing. "The weather? Why, Skye, it's a gorgeous day already. Not a scrap of cloud in the sky."

"Things change quick out here," was all Fargo said.

They resumed their northward journey to San Francisco, Fargo dividing his vigilant attention between the shuffling prisoners and the high slopes on the right. After only an hour on the trail, Cully yelled out for the second time, "Hey, Fargo! Nature calls!"

Fargo wheeled the Ovaro around. "The hell's your grift, man? We just stopped for you a half hour ago."

"Hell, I can't help it, big man. These poor victuals have give me the squitters."

Fargo cursed under his breath. Cully could be lying, but could just as well be telling the truth. The squitters, diarrhea, was more than a time-consuming nuisance. It led to weakness, dehydration; eventually Cully wouldn't be able to walk, slowing the team horses.

"I think he's faking," Newt suggested in a low tone.

"You want to go with him and verify he's faking?" Fargo offered.

Newt's fresh-scrubbed face paled. "I take your point."

"We can't keep stopping like this," Lindy fretted. "Skye, you said it would be a tight schedule even without delays."

"It'll be even tighter, sugar plum," Cully assured her, "if I get real sick. I'll have to ride in the wagon."

"You get that sick," Fargo said as he freed Cully from the lead line, "and I'm shooting you. So unless you want to rot beside the trail, you best get healthy in a hurry."

When they were back on the trail again, Newt asked, "So what's at Point Conception?"

Fargo, eyes in constant motion, shrugged one shoulder. "Nothing too special. No settlement that I know of. It's just a spot where the coast takes a little jut out to sea. Just north of there is an old Spanish mission that's being used as an Indian vocational school."

Fargo didn't bother mentioning that Point Conception was also one of the best vantage points, along the Old Mission Trail, for ambushes. Low slopes pressed close to the trail, yet were protected by sheer cliffs at their base. Nor could that deadly stretch be bypassed except by the sea.

For two hours they made steady progress with no more interruptions from Cully. They passed a shack with a strip of neglected side garden, the only sign of settlement along the trail. Some deep-rock gold was still coming down out of the Sierras. They passed an ore wagon with high wheels and a long double-team of mules. Some of the ore was so high-grade Fargo could actually see the veins of gold in it.

"No guards for that much ore?" Lindy marveled.

"Gold ore is prac'ly worthless to a bandit," Fargo told her. "It has to be taken to smelters owned by the mining companies. Back in the early days of the gold rush, there were some pure gold nuggets found weighing upwards of twenty-five pounds. Those're all gone now, and the only gold left is down in deep veins."

Fargo switched hands on the reins to rest his arms. "There's more progress for you," he said, pointing with his chin toward the rocky shoreline. Well up from the foaming surf, a surveyor stood bent over his transit, two heavily armed guards nearby.

"Is that the railroad that hired you?" Lindy asked.

"No, that one's inland more. There's several being built, sort of a race."

Fargo's matter-of-fact tone revealed nothing of his feelings, but seeing a long line of surveying pegs disturbed him. He could already visualize the iron road they'd be pushing through down here. This pristine paradise called California wouldn't stay that way for long—not after the smokestacks, deal-making fat cats, and New York land hunters flooded in. Soon enough, diamond-stack locomotives would race up and down this new state at the breakneck speed of forty miles per hour. In Fargo's view, such progress cost far more than it was worth.

"Here's what I don't get," Newt said, looking up at Fargo from the seat of the wagon. "The attack on Lindy and me in the desert, that attempt to kill all of us in Los Angeles, the attempt on Skye last night—how can anyplace be called a state for almost ten years, yet be so openly lawless?"

"It's a state, all right," Fargo replied, "but so is Missouri, and I'll guarantee you that mare's nest is lawless, too. Out here, there's a few U.S. marshals and only a small handful of soldiers to assure order. And the U.S. Army, I know from vast experience, is mostly what you'd call reactive. It spends most of its time trying to lock the stable door after the horse has been stolen."

"Man, it's rough out here, all right," Newt agreed. "Lindy and I would both be feeding worms by now, hadn't been for you, Skye. But out west at least a fellow can be a bachelor, like me and you, without being treated like a criminal. Cripes, there's *still* towns back east that levy bachelor taxes."

"If all the gals looked like your sister, Newt, towns wouldn't need any tax."

Lindy flashed him a dazzling smile, but Fargo had already turned his attention to a sharp jog in the trail just ahead—the point where it swerved west to round Point Conception. He definitely did not like that natural shooting platform east of the trail, where a brushy slope was protected by a granite cliff at its base.

"Okay, girls," he called back to the trio of dust-coated prisoners. "We're picking up the pace a little for the next few minutes. If you fall, tough shit, so stay on your feet. We're not slowing down until I say so."

He ignored their curses, looking at Newt. "Kick your team up to a trot. Lindy, hunker down in the wagon bed and pull that blanket over you."

The wagon jerked into faster motion, the prisoners cursing like stable sergeants as they were forced to a fast trot.

"But, Skye," Lindy protested, "what—?"

"Shush it and do what I told you," he snapped. "You hired me to give the orders."

Frowning, but obeying, Lindy quickly covered herself up.

"Newt," Fargo said, glancing up the cliff face on their right, "if any shots ring out, to hell with those hardcases. Just whip your team up to a fare-thee-well."

"Sure!"

Newt had figured out the trouble spot and asked no questions. The trail curved gradually seaward as they rounded the point. Waves crashed into foam along the rocky shoreline, but Fargo kept his attention on the brushy slope above them. His Henry rested on his thigh, muzzle pointing straight up, a round in the chamber.

Whenever he couldn't scout ahead, Fargo always kept a close eye on the Ovaro—the best sentry he had ever trailed with. So far the stallion had shown no signs of danger.

"Burn in hell, Fargo!" Rick Cully shouted, choking on dust. "Slow this son of a bitch down!"

"We do seem to've rounded the point," Newt remarked.

"*Please* can I come out, Skye?" Lindy pleaded from beneath the blanket. "It's terribly hot and bumpy under here."

"Yeah, c'mon out," Fargo decided, booting his rifle—not that it could have helped him, anyway. That slope was thickly covered. "We're past—"

The Ovaro's head flipped up, nostrils quivering, and Fargo felt a ball of ice replace his stomach. Lindy was still settling onto the wagon seat when Fargo kicked free of the stirrups and leaped down onto her.

Lindy screamed as Fargo pushed her back into the wagon bed only a heartbeat before Lindy's half of the board seat exploded in a spray of splinters.

10

"Whip 'em up, Newt!" Fargo shouted, still awkwardly sprawled over Lindy. "They foxed us by hiding at the very far edge of the turn. We should clear out of their angle of fire real quick."

The powerful blast of that first shot was not repeated and Fargo gave quick thanks for that—whatever the hell projectile that weapon was firing, it wouldn't take much to blow the damn wagon apart. Just then another weapon opened up—a handgun, Fargo guessed—and slugs came whiffing down like deadly hail.

"Steady on, Newt!" Fargo rallied the nerve-rattled youth even as a slug nicked a chunk out of the wagon.

The bullet-savvy Ovaro, despite the noisy racket of ambush, continued to trot alongside Fargo and the wagon. Fargo could have grabbed his Henry, but that action seemed pointless now. They had finally rounded Point Conception, and the hidden dry-gulchers had lost their angle of fire. In fact, the gunfire had ceased—*for now,* Fargo reminded himself.

"All clear," he called out, sitting up and then helping Lindy up. "Rein in for a bit, Newt."

"Jesus God Almighty!" Newt stared at the chewed-up seat beside him. "Why, Lindy wouldn't've had a snowball's chance!"

Lindy, pale as gypsum, rearranged her askew bonnet. "A bullet did that?" she asked Fargo, staring at the damage.

"No bullet I ever heard of—not even a seven-hundred grain bullet like the Sharps fires. This almost seemed to explode on impact."

"Maybe it was a shotgun?" Newt suggested.

Fargo shook his head. "A shotgun *could* do that much damage, but only at close range before the pellets can spread. It'd be prac'ly useless from up on that slope."

By now Fargo had his Arkansas toothpick out. He probed the shattered seat, finally digging out some badly damaged brass.

"Doesn't make sense," Fargo said in a musing tone, holding up the brass for Newt and Lindy to see. "This is a twenty-two cartridge. No way on God's green earth could the *bullet* do this much damage. A bigger cartridge drove it deep into the wood, and under that much pressure even a little bit of black powder explodes with great force."

Fargo glanced at the prisoners, who were being atypically quiet all of a sudden. Cully looked especially smug.

"What's with that big smile on your map, beanpole?" Fargo asked. "Bet you recognize the clever work of one of your owlhoot pals, huh? And you're thinking maybe he means to spring you?"

Cully lifted his bony shoulders, playing it cagey. "Actually, big man, I just thought it was funny. I mean, last night you topped your fancy piece and had her howling like a madwoman. Now you just topped her again in broad daylight. Horny bastard, ain'tcha?"

"Funny you should mention the woman, mouthpiece," Fargo replied. "This attack just now didn't have thing one to do with freeing you shitheels. It was an attempt to kill Miss Helzer, not to free you. So don't go tacking up bunting just yet."

Coyote made kissing noises. "That's the sound of your lips on my ass, Fargo. The worm *will* turn, crusader."

With stretched nerves they resumed their journey, Lindy forced to ride in the wagon bed now. Fargo rarely took his eyes off the mountain slopes for the rest of the day, but this stretch of the trail offered fewer vantage points for ambushers.

"Think they're done with us, Skye?" Newt asked toward late afternoon.

"No way in hell. The terrain is against them right now—brushy slopes're good for killers, but we've got screening timber now that blocks their view of the trail. Soon as it thins out, we can expect another attack."

"Any idea where that might be?" Newt pressed.

"The old La Purisima Mission, which we'll be passing tomorrow morning, is a good spot for bushwhackers. We'll also need to be especially careful about forty miles beyond it, when we reach San Luis Obispo Bay. But the attack could come anywhere, anytime."

Newt shook his head, then stared up the mountain slope. "Guess I was lulled by the scenery. This *is* a dangerous stretch."

"It's no trek for a worrywart," Fargo agreed.

He glanced at Lindy. "I know you're sworn to silence. But I think I've pretty much put it together. This Wagner fellow you're trying to stop . . . last time I was in San Francisco, there was a jasper named Prescott Wagner lording it over the place. Had the Hounds eating out of his hand. I'd bet my horse he's the one trying to kill you. I'm thinking November first is a court date, and you're testifying against him. And somehow it involves your sister Belinda and her death."

"I can't answer any of that, Skye," Lindy said. "But let's just say . . . you're as intelligent as you are handsome."

"Intelligent?" Rick Cully gave that one a hoot. "If he's so damned intelligent, sugar britches, what's he doin' haulin' *us* around when he ain't got no chance in hell of turning us in? A man with any brains wouldn't be on this fool's mission."

Fargo ignored the barb, but in fact Cully had a point, he realized. Somehow, Fargo was always setting out to earn a few dollars by honest work; inevitably, he ended up picking lead out of his sitter.

"Why do you keep staring at the sky?" Lindy asked Fargo. "It's deep blue with hardly any clouds."

"Past couple hours I've noticed rabbits and other animals heading to high ground," Fargo replied. "I've got a God fear there's a flash flood coming. And this is the worst place to be when it hits."

Newt and Lindy exchanged amused glances.

"Rabbits?" Newt repeated. "They're as dumb as hens."

" 'S'matter, Fargo?" Coyote chipped in. "Bunions aching?"

"I could be wrong," Fargo admitted in a mild tone. "Let's hope so."

They traveled without further incident until a half hour before sunset. Good camping spots were rare now, so Fargo led them right down to the spot where the tree line met the rocky shoreline of the Pacific.

As soon as the prisoners were secured to trees for the night, Fargo turned to caring for the Ovaro. Using a horseshoe nail, he carefully pried out pebbles and thorns embedded in the stallion's hooves.

Lindy, busy boiling beans, called over to Fargo, "I've noticed you and that horse of yours. Sometimes he seems to respond to your will with no commands whatsoever."

Fargo opened his mouth to reply, but eager bookworm Newt beat him to it.

"That's the way of it out west, sis. You'll read about it in any book or magazine article about the frontier. See, no man can truly be respected out here if he can't manage a horse. Right, Skye?"

Fargo grinned at the kid's zeal. " 'Ain't no horse that can't be rode, ain't no man that can't be throwed.' "

Coyote was tied up at least fifty yards away in the trees, but he had the hearing of a civet cat.

" 'At's right, Fargo!" he bellowed. "Ain't *no* man that can't be throwed. Includin' you. So let us go now and make it easy on yourself, anh? Hell, I like you."

Fargo looked at Newt, speaking quietly. "They're wanted in San Francisco, and despite all their bluff and bluster they know they'll stretch hemp if we get them there. We need to watch them close."

"You said it's lawless in San Francisco," Newt pointed out. "So what's for them to fear?"

"Plenty. With California a state now, they have to come into the fold. San Francisco has a new prosecutor, assuming he ain't been shot. These owlhoots have all been officially indicted. True, the vigilantes still ride roughshod over the city, but they've toned it down lately and concentrate on Mexicans and Chinese since they ain't protected by U.S. law. These three *will* swing. Others have."

Fargo put the Ovaro on a long tether as he added, "We'll be switching off on guard as usual. Walk over and check on those hardcases at least every fifteen minutes."

When supper was ready, Newt propped up the tailgate of the wagon with sticks, making a table.

As usual, Newt made a dour face over his bland meal of beans and hardtack. "You know, Skye," he said wistfully, "Lindy gets up a tasty supper of fried grits and side meat. *This* slop isn't fit for hogs."

Fargo was busy spooning food, eating with evident gusto. "If you've gone hungry enough times," he told Newt, "you learn to appreciate even poor rations. I spent ten days once living on slippery elm bark and acorns. Then I got a hankering for a hot meal and boiled my buckskins."

"Any decent food in San Francisco?" Lindy asked.

Fargo nodded. "Plenty. They like to live high on the hog there. Got chefs from New Orleans, Paris, even Samoa."

"I know what *I* want," Newt said on a sigh. "And it doesn't require a fancy chef. Steak, biscuits, potatoes with gravy, greens, and apple pie for dessert."

Fargo stayed his hand when Newt started to dump his uneaten beans. "I'll take that, Newt. Waste not, want not."

By now the sun was a glowing orange sphere balanced just above the dark and heaving swells of the ocean. Fargo and Newt filled three plates and walked back to the tree line to untie the prisoners so they could eat.

"How 'bout it, Fargo?" Cully wheedled the moment they arrived. "Play it smart for once and save your ass. Just turn us loose tonight and your troubles are over."

"You got it bass-ackwards," Fargo corrected him. "*Your* troubles would be over, not mine. Me, I'd have to live with the fact that I turned three woman-killers loose on society. That ain't *worth* saving my ass. Besides . . ."

Fargo glanced at the next tree to the left, where the brooding, taciturn Stone Lofley was tied up. "You boys got a date with the hangman in San Francisco—ain't that right, Lofley?"

"A buncha goddamn wimmin jack their jaws," Lofley growled. "Just gimme my food, Fargo."

"You'll sure as shit rue this night, Fargo!" Cully's angry voice hollered behind Fargo and Newt as they returned to the wagon parked on the beach. "What happened today was just a *taste* of what's comin'—you hear me, cock chafer?"

"He's right on one point," Fargo said quietly to Newt. "The worst is yet to come. But springing these curs won't

104

save us—it's your sister Wagner's dirt workers have to kill. *Whoa!*"

Fargo stopped dead in his tracks, amazed at the sight before them in the moonlight. Sometimes, from frustration, women traveling along the remote Western trails would don their best silk-and-lace gowns in the evening, bustles and crinolines included. Lindy stood before them in a pinch-waisted, emerald green gown swollen out by hoops.

"Like it?" Lindy asked, twirling around.

"I like it just fine," Fargo assured her. "Matter fact, it's a reg'lar tonic just looking at you, pretty lady."

Fargo glanced into the hidebound trunk she had opened: fine French muslin, satin slippers and gloves, more gowns of taffeta and lace. He could smell the fragrant sachets she had packed in with her best clothing and linen.

"Just curious," he said. "There's a brand-new Butterfield Express stagecoach service from Saint Louis to San Francisco. Fast, too. Makes the trip in twenty-five days. You two ain't hauling much property, so why didn't you take it?"

"Costs too damn much, Skye," Newt replied. "More than the city of San Francisco could—"

"Newt!" Lindy interrupted, and her brother flushed.

Fargo laughed, shaking his head. "You two need a little practice at lying. Don't worry. I'll ask no more questions. I already figured out that San Francisco's new prosecutor was paying your way."

"Anyhow," Newt said, "tickets are more than three hundred dollars *apiece*. We're not poor, but that's almost a year's wages where I come from."

"And meals," Lindy added, "are three dollars each. Back home that would buy twelve restaurant meals."

Fargo whistled. "I heard it was dear. Didn't know you had to be an Astor to afford it."

"Indian burner?" Newt offered the bottle of Kentucky bourbon to Fargo.

"A smooth distillation," Fargo praised before he tipped the bottle back.

"What's wrong?" Lindy implored in a nervous tone when Fargo lowered the bottle without drinking. He stared intently into the night sky, his features grim.

"See that circle around the moon?" he asked. "That means rain before morning."

Newt chuckled. "Even if it does, Skye, so what? The world would cease to flourish without rain. Cripes, there's more misery caused by drought than by rain."

Fargo shook his head at Newt's know-it-all tone. "It's no crime to aid and abet an idiot, I s'pose. Newt, the three of us are trapped on a narrow plain between steep mountains and the Pacific Ocean. Even a couple hours of heavy rain can turn this strip into a raging torrent. And we got no place to run to."

Fargo saw the wink Newt sent to his sister.

"No offense, Skye," he said in a condescending tone one might use with a difficult child. "But Lindy and I both grew up on a farm. Your trail skills are very impressive, but nobody knows rain better than farmers. That sky is cloudless—*look* at all those stars!"

Fargo let the argument die. He never pushed if a thing wouldn't move. It hardly mattered if Newt and Lindy believed him. They'd find out soon enough the difference between a planting rain in Illinois and a killing rain in California.

"*Psst!* Hey, Rick! Rick, wake up, boy!"

Cully, his body exhausted from another long day spent trotting behind the wagon, woke up only gradually. When his eyelids finally quivered open, sudden elation made his heart sing.

The furtive face of Lumpy Neck McGuire stared down at him in the silvery-white moonlight.

"Lumpy? Christ, am I—?"

Lumpy Neck cursed in a whisper, slapping a hand over his fellow criminal's mouth.

"Keep your damn voice down, you fool. Took me hours to crawl through these trees. Fargo is on sentry, and that bastard can hear thoughts."

"Sure, sure, sorry. C'mon, cut us loose so we can pull foot outta here."

Lumpy Neck shook his head. "Pull foot how? I'm with Jack Slade, who don't know I'm here, and we got only two horses. Besides, I can't cut Stone or Coyote loose—their trees are better lit by the firelight. And the way Fargo's keepin' that fire stoked, he must be suspicious."

"Well, hell, at least cut *me* loose. I can steal a horse from someone on the trail."

"Yeah, but think it through. I cut your ropes, and the next time Fargo walks over here, what happens? He sees you're gone, and he's instantly warned. That leaves Stone and Coyote up shit creek without a paddle."

Cully felt sudden anger heat his face. "You ain't cuttin' me loose? Jesus Christ with a wooden dick! So what's this—just stopped by to tuck me in?"

"Slade sent me out with strict orders *just* to scout. He's got a hair up his ass about capturing Fargo alive, then layin' a fiery whip to him 'fore he puts his head on display in a ar—I think he said a jar."

Cully was so infuriated that a murderous rage filled him. 'Jar, can, pedestal, who gives a shit? Slade is a goddamn madman! A man can't get fancy with a widow maker like Fargo, Lumpy. You just kill him from cover—cover just ike these trees, anh?"

"Sure, and I was hoping to kill him," Lumpy Neck insisted. "That's why I'm here. I been a long time waitin' for ust the chance, but that cunning bastard suspects he's in he crosshairs. See how he always turns sideways to these rees, and keeps his eyes on this spot constantly? I can't drill him at this distance or get closer without him seein' ne."

"He comes close to check on us pretty reg'lar," Cully pointed out. "Why'n't you plug him then?"

"Because I'd hafta be right here at the edge to get a clear shot through the trees. But that son of a bitch has night vision like a cat."

Cully cursed again. "So me, Coyote and Stone are going o dance on air in 'Frisco, just on accounta you ain't got he stones to kill Fargo?"

Lumpy Neck's sudden scowl made Cully regret his peppery tongue.

"The lanky bastard ain't got *me* tied to a tree, has he?" Lumpy Neck retorted. "But never mind all that—I *am* going to spring you boys. And it's a better, smarter plan han just trying to kill Fargo from ambush."

Lumpy Neck pulled a Colt Pocket Model from his sash. "You'll never sneak up on Fargo—men have died hard trying that. But *any* man can be killed through the element of surprise."

Cully was tied twice: to the tree and at the wrists. Lumpy Neck pulled his big bowie knife from its belt sheath and sawed through the ropes on Cully's wrists.

"He has to come back and untie you in the morning," Slade explained. "Being a savvy and careful type, he'll untie your big ropes first. Then he'll have to come in close to free your hands. Just hide the cut part of the ropes. That Colt Pocket is small—just hide it 'tween your legs and plug the bastard."

A wide grin tugged Cully's lips apart. "Slicker 'n snot on a doorknob, Lumpy. Then I can kill that greenhorn brother before he even wakes up. And with him and Fargo planted, the girl will be shit outta luck."

Cully paused, then added, "Of course, Jack won't like it none—not if he's hungry to take Judge Lash to Fargo's hide before the bastard's killed. But I'll cut off his head and give it to Slade as a peace offering. That son of a bitch Fargo tossed me to the grizzlies, and he *will* die for it."

Lumpy Neck nodded, nervous eyes still watching Fargo. He seemed to be gazing into the sky an awful lot. Lumpy Neck wondered, for a moment, if the crashing waves of the Pacific seemed to be growing louder. The wind was sure's hell picking up, and heavy raindrops were pattering the leaves.

"All that sounds all right," he finally told Cully. "The Helzer woman is the main mile. Fargo has to be croaked, too, or the vengeful bastard will track and kill all of us. But that pert skirt could lob some nasty bombs in court. You know how jurors are when a pretty gal testifies under oath—it's got the force of Gospel. You've got to finish the job you boys started. Kill that mouthy bitch."

Cully, busy secreting the Colt between his thighs, nodded forcefully. "She's pretendin' not to, but she does recognize Stone. He's the one that held her at gunpoint while Wagner done for her sister."

"Damn! Here comes Fargo to check on you three," Lumpy Neck fretted, beginning to fade back into the trees. "Make sure that rope looks tied, and start snoring. It's best to wait until morning, when he has to lean in close. But if he acts one bit suspicious, plug him, Rick—don't wait until morning if surprise is on your side."

Fargo's attention had been divided all night between the dark mass of the trees and the increasing signs of a storm making up. It was time to turn the last shift of guard duty over to Newt, but first he needed to look in on the sleeping prisoners.

Lindy was asleep in the bed of the wagon, Newt under it. As Fargo crossed the beach toward the trees, the brisk, cool night wind picked up to a powerful gust. Fargo had to seize his hat at one point, and moonlight over the ocean showed whitecaps forming. The rain was not yet heavy, but the stiff wind sent the drops pelting into Fargo's face like buckshot.

The rain's coming, Fargo thought, *and all hell's coming with it.*

Brilliant white tines of lightning forked the sky, followed by a long rumble of thunder. As he neared the shadowy trees, Fargo slowed his pace and filled his hand with blued steel. These trees were easily accessible from behind, and Fargo knew damn good and well there were thugs trying to free this trio of scum buckets.

Another bone white spiderweb of lightning, another rolling crash of loud thunder. The big fire Fargo had built on the beach was still surviving the rain. Fargo glanced in at Stone Lofley and Coyote first.

Both men had been woken by the thunder. Lofley simply stared at his captor, his brooding face promising a hard death at the first chance. Coyote chuckled the moment he spotted Fargo.

"You finally done bulling your white squaw?" the Apache roweled Fargo. "Bring that big-tit bitch back here. Nobody misses a slice off a cut loaf."

Fargo shook his head in disbelief at the man's depravity. As he started toward Cully's tree, Coyote called out behind him.

"You see that ocean, Fargo, starting to toss like a wild mustang? Feel that wind? We're *all* gonna die, Fargo, you stupid bastard! You've mounted your last mare, stud!"

Fargo despised the murdering scut, but Coyote was pure-quill Apache and knew bad weather, all right. As Fargo walked closer to Cully's tree, the lightning and thunder became almost constant, lighting the trees up like bright afternoon.

Cully appeared to be fast asleep and snoring up a racket like a buffalo with a head cold. Fargo leathered his Colt and started to return to camp, then froze in place.

Something was wrong. Then he realized what it was. The noise of the storm, plus all the brilliant lightning, had woken the other two, and twice Coyote had raised his voice to a shout. Yet, with all that racket, Cully was sound asleep?

"Something ain't jake," Fargo muttered, shucking out his Colt again. This time he thumbed back the hammer.

He crept slowly back. Sure enough the snoring had stopped. When Fargo was close enough to be spotted in the almost continuous lightning, it suddenly flashed again, turning night into day.

Fargo could see Cully clearly, and there was something suspicious about the way his hands were thrust between his thighs. However, the ropes appeared to be tied.

"Either you're playing with yourself," Fargo said out loud, still guessing, "or you're hiding a weapon. Which is it?"

It was Fargo's way to take a bull by the horns, not chase after its tail. He knelt down, found a rock big enough to fill his hand, then waited until the next flash of lightning.

"Heads up, Cully!" he shouted, flinging the rock right at the thug's chest.

It was good reflexes that sent Cully across the Great Divide. Spotting the rock, he lifted both freed hands to catch it before it smashed into him.

He slapped the rock aside, cursing when he realized how Fargo had tricked him. Even now Fargo waited, unwilling to kill a possibly unarmed man. Cully sealed his own fate when his right hand snapped up with the Colt Pocket blazing.

He managed to snap off a wildly aimed bullet before Fargo's Colt leaped into his fist. The first shot was low and tore away most of Cully's lower jaw. The man's blood-spraying scream of agony made Fargo wince because he always tried for a clean, quick kill. His second slug punched into Cully's forehead, and the hardcase slumped dead.

Lindy woke up screaming at the gunshots. Newt shouted at Fargo, "You okay, Skye?"

"I'm fine!" he shouted back. "Trouble's over!"

However, Fargo knew, as he felt the rain start to drill its way earthward with steady force, that the serious trouble was just now beginning—trouble he couldn't outshoot, throw ropes around, or beat into submission with his fists. Trouble that had reduced even the toughest of frontier denizens to mere floating debris.

A flash flood was about to engulf them, and on the California coast that was the closest thing to a death sentence.

11

The racket of gunfire had abated, but the fury of the storm quickly dwarfed it. The rain pelted down so fiercely that sleep was out of the question. Fargo lent his oilskin slicker to Lindy and found himself soaked to the skin in minutes.

"I know it's still dark out," Lindy said with a nervous tremor in her voice. "But—but shouldn't we leave this area immediately?"

"That's a tough call," Fargo admitted, straining to be heard above the storm-tossed ocean and the rain now hurtling down in almost solid sheets. "Good chance there's no place to go to because of the size of this storm—and even if we did leave, only way we could run is north or south. Might be best to ride it out right here."

He found a stick, carved five notches in it about two inches apart, and headed back out to the trail. His heart sank when Fargo discovered the trail had already become a fast-running stream. He jammed the stick into the remaining ground, noting that four notches showed above the churning flood water.

"Skye, I'm *so* sorry," Lindy greeted him when he came back to the wagon. "About mocking you, I mean, when you said a flash flood might be coming."

"Me, too, Skye," Newt said, now so soaked he looked like a half-drowned puppy. "All that crap about how farmers know weather best."

Fargo impatiently waved all of this off.

"Who's wrong or right ain't the issue right now," he told both of them. "It's about living or dying. This heavy rain just might stop soon. Or it might keep up for hours. If it

oes, our only hope is to get to higher ground fast. Other-
ise, we'll be washed out to sea."

"Higher ground?" Newt said uncertainly. "Skye, that
ope beside the trail is steep. Sometimes it even turns to
iffs. I can see *us* getting up there somehow, maybe, but
ot the team and the wagon."

"And without the team and wagon, how will we reach
an Francisco on time?" Lindy asked in a tone on the verge
f panic. "Skye, I *must* be there by—"

"I know, I know," Fargo said wearily. Why were all the
uicide missions dumped into *his* lap? "You just hafta be
ere by November first or it's too late. Why'n't you put a
ine to it?"

"Sorry."

Her forlorn manner softened Fargo's heart. He patted
er face, across which rivulets of water zigzagged crazily.

"We'll get you up there," Fargo promised. "I got a hunch
uat what you're doing is mighty important stuff. Be right
ack."

Eyes blinded by driving rain, Fargo hurried back out to
ue trail to check his water gauge.

"Hell and furies," he said aloud after bending down to
ook at the stick. Four notches were showing when he'd
lanted it about twenty minutes ago. Now only three
otches showed, the third just barely. Fargo watched it for
 minute and saw water ebb quickly higher, swallowing
ue mark.

He splashed back to the wagon. "Hitch the team," he
rdered Newt and Lindy in a take-charge voice. "We have
 get to higher ground *now* or it'll be too late. This is one
ell of a gully washer."

The Helzers were too damn scared to ask any questions.
hey set to work while Fargo quickly rigged his stallion.
he Ovaro had survived so many rough scrapes, in so many
fferent regions, that bad weather was barely more than a
uisance. The dray team pulling the wagon, however, were
 the verge of bolting in panic.

With the Ovaro tacked, Fargo moved back toward the
vo surviving prisoners. Almost constant lightning revealed
ully's dead body, slumped against his ropes. Fargo
ouldn't help wondering who gave him that Colt Pocket,
nd just how far away he or they were. Solving that little

mystery, however, would have to wait. Right now there was a deluge to survive.

Fargo knelt beside Cully's body long enough to remove the badly needed ropes. He left the body jackknifed against the tree and tossed the Colt into the bushes—Fargo's party did not lack for weapons, and carrying extras was too much risk with killers to transport.

"Well, no shit, Fargo!" Coyote bellowed when the Trails man showed up. "Now it's time to murder me 'n' Stone just like you done for Rick, anh? You cunning son of a bitch. Shoulda used that pigsticker of yours, we'da never knowed."

"Cully begged for it," Fargo said, kneeling down to untie the Apache's ropes after first checking his hands carefully. "When a gun is aimed at me, I tend to take it personal for some crazy reason."

"Don't blow smoke up my ass, Fargo. Rick had no barking iron."

"All right, let's say I did murder the mangy cur. You two knotheads want me to think that asshole's death is misting you up?"

Coyote, his "indignation" less evident now, said, "You're a loner, Fargo, a one-man outfit. You got a heart chipped from flint. But me, Stone, and Rick, see, we rode a lot of trails together."

"Oh, Jesus, give it a rest," Fargo said, shaking his head at the man's sheer audacity. "*I* got a heart of flint? Coyote, I know for a fact you scalped your own family for the bounty. Both of you barn rats have been murdering, raping and stealing for years. Come hell or high water"—Fargo paused, realizing the high water was here—"I'll bring you two before the bar of justice."

"Cully and us was blood brothers," Coyote insisted stubbornly. "The three musketeers. Stone will bear me out on that, right, Stone?"

Lofley, unaffected by the pouring rain or Coyote's phony sentimentality, shifted onto one cheek and farted loudly. "Kiss for ya, Fargo," he said through a leering grin.

He glanced over at his companion in crime. "And screw you, Coyote, you sniveling coward. Far as Cully—the three musketeers, my ass. I've picked better men than him outta chicken shit. I ain't scairt a Fargo and I aim to kill him real soon now."

Fargo didn't show it, in the flickering lightning, but brutally frank Stone Lofley made him nervous. The Trailsman had met plenty of men out west, most of them decent. Some, especially veterans of the Mexican War, had caught the kill fever and lost any regard for human life. Stone, however, made even *these* men look like saints.

"Cully will soon be sailing the high seas," Fargo snapped, stepping back quickly after he finished untying both sets of ropes. He held his Colt on the pair. "Now lissenup if you don't want to drown. I'm going to tie both of you together at the waist, but your hands will be left free so you can climb."

"Climb what?" Coyote demanded.

"You'll find out soon enough," Fargo replied, herding them before him. "One sign of a fox play, and you'll join your 'blood brother' in hell."

Out on the trail, conditions were rapidly deteriorating, and Fargo felt a cold tongue of fear lick at his belly. He could stand tall in the face of a gunfighter, but no man could whip nature's fury into submission.

And this, Fargo realized as he bent his head low against the driving rain, was furious. By the time they managed to goad the reluctant team into motion, Fargo's stick was completely covered with swirling water. Water also poured off the slope beside the trail, threatening to unleash a killer mudslide at any moment.

"Jesus, Skye!" a nervous Newt shouted above the racket of the storm. He grabbed the whip from its socket and gave the rebellious wheelhorse a cut across the flanks. "I can feel the wagon actually starting to float at times. Won't be long, that water'll just take it out to sea."

Fargo nodded. Since slow going was the only option, he had tied his Ovaro to the tailgate for now. Coyote and Lofley trudged behind the wagon, Fargo covering them on foot. The water level was creeping over his calves.

"It *will* float off soon," Fargo shouted back. "But we need to get a little farther down the trail. The slope is too steep right here, but that's our only hope."

"You ain't gettin' this heavy wagon up that slope," Coyote mocked. "Even you ain't God, Fargo."

Fargo paid scant attention to the Apache, watching Stone

Lofley intently. Lofley kept catching Fargo's eye and grinning like the demented killer he was.

"It's not letting up, Skye," Lindy called back to Fargo her voice on the edge of panic. "The trail's becoming a fast river!"

Fargo was at least grateful it was October. Many of California's rivers became raging torrents in season, especially those that flowed out of the Sierra swollen with snowmelt Even so, right now there were torrents of water washing down onto the coastal plain, and Fargo wasn't seeing much change in the steep angle of the slope.

Within mere minutes Fargo and the prisoners were splashing through fast water almost up to their knees, and starting to stagger in their fight against the strong current

"Oh, Jerusalem!" Newt shouted. "There she goes!"

He meant the tail end of the wagon, which suddenly floated sideways. The Ovaro nickered in angry protest and resisted the pull, muscles impressive in the blue-white flashes of lightning. His efforts and the weight of the floundering team up front kept the vehicle more or less on the trail—not that any trail was even visible.

"All right, Newt, kick the brake on," Fargo ordered "This is as far as we dare to go."

Keeping a close eye on the two hardcases, whose hand were temporarily free, Fargo braced his shoulder against one side of the solid wooden wagon and forced it to the right bank of the trail, where the water wasn't quite so deep or fast.

"Unhitch the team," he told Newt, taking off his hat to shake water out of the curled brim. "But don't let those horses get away—they'll try to bolt."

"The hell you up to, Fargo?" Coyote demanded. "That' damn near a *wall* next to us, not no slope. You ain't gettin that mother-ruttin' wagon up there. The world will grow honest first."

"I ain't getting it up there," Fargo agreed. "But *we* are.'

"Eat shit and go naked, Fargo!" Lofley spat out, ange causing him to break his habitual silence yet again. "Here you are, takin' us to 'Frisco so we can hang. And you think we're gonna help you do it?"

Even the rain streaming over his face couldn't soften Fargo's menacing stare. He thumbed back the hammer of

is Colt and leveled it at Lofley's gut—close enough to
owder burn his shirt. In the intermittent bursts of lighting, Fargo looked like some fierce avenging angel.

"Is that your final answer?" he asked. " 'Cause if it is,
'm puttin' the bullet about two inches below your belly
utton. It'll shred your entrails and hurt like nothin' you
ver felt before. And the best part—you'll need between
welve and twenty-four hours to bleed to death internally,
creaming your head off the whole time."

Lofley's face crumpled with mindless rage. "Up yours,
o-gooder! *No* man buffaloes Stone Lofley."

"Your choice," Fargo reminded him in a mild tone. His
nger curled inside the trigger guard.

"Wait!" Lofley shouted, fear replacing his hotheaded
nger. "Don't shoot, damn your eyes! I'll help."

Fargo swung the Colt's muzzle over to Coyote. "How
out you, red son of the mission schools? You on this
orking party?"

"I'll kill you another time," Coyote replied. "Let's turn
is wagon into a mountain goat."

Newt, Fargo noticed, was having one hell of a time with
is team horses, both of which were unhitched and bucking.
nly the churning water, which scared them, kept them
om bolting away.

"They're too wild to be of any use to us," Fargo told
e struggling Newt. "But we have to gentle them enough
 get them up the slope and tied off. Then, using my stal-
on as the main muscle, we're going to rope that wagon
nd drag it up the slope."

Newt didn't look too convinced this could ever be done
y mortal men. He also seemed to understand there
eren't many alternate plans of action. Fargo was glad he
ad seized all their ropes when he collared the owlhoots
own in the Mojave Desert. Working quickly, for the water
as still rising fast, he tied several ropes together after first
ving some knots in each of them for handholds.

"Cover the prisoners," he told Newt, handing him the
enry. "Christ sakes, don't tolerate anything from them.
atch 'em both like a cat on rats. If in doubt, shoot."

Relying on everything he'd ever learned about terrain
nd topography, Fargo splashed up and down along the
ase of the slope, looking for the best spot. By dint of sheer

will and muscle, he scaled the almost liquid, almost vertical base. As he ascended, ripping loose fingernails to claw those first, desperate yards, he tied his guide rope to trees or strong roots.

Not too far up the slope Fargo struck good fortune: a dry cavern sheltered by a limestone overhang and roughly the size of a ballroom. He searched it quickly and found no bears or wildcats within. With his guide rope to ease the climb, Fargo scrambled nimbly down.

"You okay, Newt?" he shouted above the din.

The tenderfoot held the Henry aimed at the prisoners. Coyote and Lofley were soaked to the skin, cold, and realized this was no time to spring a break—where would they go? The antediluvian flood tended to make even the toughest men feel powerless. They sat on the tailgate, looking like sailors after a failed mutiny.

"I guess I'm okay," Newt said, as miserable and scared as his prisoners. "Now I understand why all the help wanted notices out west always say 'orphans preferred.' "

Fargo gave Newt's shoulder a squeeze for encouragement. "Hang in there, lumberjack. We've got good shelter up on the slope. I'm taking Lindy up now, then your team. After that, us four men and my stallion will drag that wagon up."

Newt was shivering hard now, not listening close. Hating to do it, Fargo slapped his face. "Damn it, listen. Those two shitbirds don't look so feisty right now, but they *will* kill you in one puffin' hurry if you go puny for even a second."

Lindy tried to remain plucky, but fear, the rain, cold, and wind had numbed her to near stupefaction like Newt. Fargo put a strong embrace around her from behind and led her up to the cavern, sometimes forced to carry both of them. When she was safely tucked inside, Fargo went down for the team horses. They were strong dray stock, and Fargo was confident they could master that slope—but only if they could be gentled enough to follow commands.

Up north in the Snake River country of Hell's Canyon, Fargo's trapper friend Snowshoe Hendee had taught him a useful trick for gentling panicked horses. He grabbed the wheelhorse by its neck halter and it shied back, hunkering on its hocks. The moment Fargo got a blindfold over its eyes the gelding quit fighting.

The Trailsman quickly placed his mouth over the horse's nostrils and breathed in gently. The gelding was still plenty nervous, but now responded to commands. Fargo quickly gave the same treatment to the other horse.

"Hey, Fargo," Coyote said after watching this impressive display. "You raise the dead, too?"

"Once I fill a grave, Messy, I leave it filled."

Despite his bravado, Fargo felt the presence of death like a man beside him. Stone Lofley was on the verge of erupting like a fumarole, Fargo felt it. Also, whoever smuggled that gun to Cully was likely nearby. Opportunities for attack would be plentiful, especially if Fargo failed to save the wagon and team.

Which he strained mightily to do now. He had gained the trust of both horses, and they followed him through the churning water, now three feet deep across the trail and flowing with powerful force. Twice Fargo almost went down, saving himself by grabbing at his rope.

"Easy goes it," he kept repeating to the frightened, wide-eyed horses, leading them up the slope by their halter ropes.

They gave it a mighty effort, but the water-drenched rope offered little purchase. Fargo shook a full oat bag from in front, and that did the trick. Once the two horses had scrambled about twenty feet up, the slope evened out a bit and they quickly reached the cave.

"Company coming, lady," Fargo called, hazing the horses inside.

Normally a horse would refuse to enter an unfamiliar enclosure like this. With a raging torrent outside, however, they seemed grateful for the dry shelter.

"Believe me," Lindy assured Fargo, nodding toward the horses. "As for company, I'll take this pair over those two abominations in the wagon any day."

"Speaking of the wagon . . . here comes the hard part," Fargo said, reluctantly returning into the teeth of the storm.

With Newt still covering the prisoners, Fargo rigged a rope collar to the wagon tongue, tying that to his saddle horn. Two more ropes were tied to tow rings on both sides of the frame. By now lightning was constant, and tornadic wind gusts forced Fargo to bend almost double.

"My horse will carry the main load," he shouted to the

119

others. "But until that wagon clears the steep base, he'l[l] need help. *Every* man will pull and pull hard."

"Fargo, has your brain gone soft?" Coyote asked, eyein[g] the slope. "How high we gotta take this heavy mother?"

"Not far," Fargo promised. "Soon as it's in the clea[r] from rising water we'll just tie it off on trees. I want Coyot[e] and Newt on one rope, me and Stone on the other. And sure's hell better see every man's muscles straining hard— remember what Cully got."

Fargo had left enough slack in the ropes to allow eac[h] man to climb up past the steepest part. First he sent New[t] up as guard, then the two prisoners. Next he brought th[e] Ovaro up to join them, and the hernia fest began.

The stalwart Ovaro pulled mightily, often losing his foot[t]ing on the saturated slope. Exhorting the others with [a] mixture of curses and encouragement, Fargo dug in hi[s] heels, leaned almost horizontally, and strained his muscle[s] until they stood out like taut cables.

"Lofley, you goddamn shirker!" he growled throug[h] clenched teeth. "Pull your freight, mister, or feed the worms!"

Fargo and Newt had been forced to put their weapon[s] away while they labored. Fargo quickly snubbed his rope t[o] a tree and shucked out his short iron, leveling it on Lofle[y].

"I've had my belly full of you, you ugly, murdering, whin[n]ing son of a bitch," Fargo shouted above the roar of fo[ul] weather and angry ocean. "Now this is your last warnin[g] either carry your weight or you die of colic—*lead* colic."

Fargo stood about fifteen feet above Lofley on steep muddy slope. Abruptly, the saturated ground beneath hi[m] gave way like quicksand, and Fargo did a backwards somer[r]sault as he lost all footing.

Fear knotted his insides when Fargo, still in midair, los[t] his hold on the Colt.

A feral roar of triumph rose from Lofley as he droppe[d] his rope and lunged wildly for the revolver now slidin[g] down toward him. Fargo landed hard on his back, but lik[e] a fighting cat he bounced reflexively to his feet.

"Too goddamn late, you crusading son of a bitch!" Lofley roared in triumph as he pointed the Colt at Farg[o]. "Chew on *this*!"

Fargo never gave up any fight until it was over. Howeve[r]

Lofley stood at point-blank range with little chance of missing. As Fargo launched himself the final few feet, his body warned itself that death had finally arrived.

The Colt fired, but with an oddly muffled sound. Chunks of mud slapped Fargo's chest, stinging little more than wind-driven gravel. He realized, just before his weight and momentum bowled Lofley over, what had happened: the sliding gun had gotten mud jammed into its muzzle. That wasn't enough to stop the bullet, but it veered wildly off course.

Stone Lofley was a powerfully built man, but Fargo had rage and frustration on his side. A fist like a cedar mallet sent Lofley reeling when Fargo's powerful haymaker caught him flush. Fargo enjoyed the sound of Lofley's teeth clacking like dice. Nonetheless, he restrained his anger for now, realizing Newt and Coyote were on the verge of exhaustion. Fargo pulled the hardcase to his feet, recovering the Colt and holstering it.

"Pull or die," Fargo said quietly, sliding the Arkansas toothpick from his boot. "It's past talk now."

Lofley's surly, piglike eyes stared at the long, thin, lethally honed blade in the generous moonlight. Without a word, he picked up his end of the rope. Only five minutes later the wagon was securely snubbed to several strong trees.

By the time they reached the cavern, Fargo was in for a pleasant surprise. Lindy had found plenty of dry firewood and had a cheery blaze going. Fargo tied up the prisoners securely and let them sit near the fire to dry their clothing. Even with three horses hobbled at one side of the cavern, there was plenty of room.

"You okay?" Fargo asked Lindy, for earlier she appeared to be at the end of her tether.

She nodded. Streaks in her blond hair glowed almost gold in the firelight. "I think so, but only because you were there to take charge. I've never in my life experienced weather like this or even dreamed it existed. A flood back home may get deep and destructive, all right, but it takes days, weeks—not *minutes*."

"You're not in Illinois," Fargo agreed, yawning. All his exertions on the slope had left his muscles hot and aching.

"Lindy likes to read penny dreadfuls," Newt chipped in. "We use to laugh at how the characters are always being 'rendered witless by terror.' Now I know it's no cliché."

Coyote laughed. "Terror? You dirt-scratchin' dough bellies ain't seen nothing yet. Smartest goddamn thing you can do is let me and Stone go while you haul your lily white asses back home. All you'll find out here is an early grave."

Fargo was dog tired, all right, but not to the point of stupidity. Before he spread his blanket and groundsheet, he carefully inspected the ropes binding Lofley and Coyote. Fortunately, they too were exhausted and would probably need to sleep.

Since his failure earlier to kill Fargo on the slope, Lofley had grown more talkative—even friendly, in the manner of a snake.

"Wise up, Fargo," he urged while the Trailsman carefully snugged all his knots one last time. "A man bends with the breeze or he breaks. Out here there's money to toss at the birds. A man like you could be a strong right arm to, say, Prescott Wagner."

"Considering the uses a right arm is put to," Fargo replied, standing up, "I b'lieve I'll pass. Besides, I got a hunch me and Wagner will be settling some accounts."

"All right, but I gave you a chance."

"You had a chance, too," Fargo reminded him. "A chance to work an honest job and be a decent citizen. Now you'll hang."

"Ain't nothin' gonna hurt us," Coyote interjected. When his hands were free he had removed his leather headband to let his long black hair dry. "*Nothin',* you savvy? We got friends out here."

"So I hear. Like Prescott Wagner, right? But there's no honor among thieves. His days are numbered, and so are yours. Vermin can't thrive once a place catches a spark of decency."

Coyote gave that a sneering hoot. "In a pig's ass, you goddamn fool! Me 'n' Stone are gonna turn California into our personal whore. And you, Fargo, are gonna buy the farm, bull and all."

"I'll live to piss on your grave," Fargo said with quiet confidence before he walked away.

The rain was finally tapering off. Lindy, utterly exhausted, had fallen asleep fully dressed. Fargo tossed a blanket over her.

"I'll take the first watch, Newt," he told the exhausted youth. "I'll roust you awake in two hours."

The rain let up completely within the next hour and the sky began to lighten. Fargo, seated cross-legged just inside the cave entrance, Henry across his thighs, let out a low whistle—he could hear the flood waters rushing by below on the trail with the force of a swift river. Damn good thing they took the trouble to seek high ground, he realized, or else they'd all be on their way to Hawaii.

The end of one battle, however, usually marked the beginning of the next, for Fargo. This very night someone had sneaked into camp below on the beach and slipped Rick Cully a gun. Obviously, or so Fargo figured, Lindy was appearing in court on November first with some kind of bombshell that could blow Prescott Wagner's criminal empire to smithereens. This mess was far from over.

A second hour passed, and a new problem presented itself. Mosquitoes were always a problem after any hard rain. They were becoming sheer hell after the flood, attacking the occupants of the cave with a demonic fury.

One by one, all four sleepers woke up, Coyote and Lofley cursing loudest because they couldn't slap at the tormenting insects.

"Jesus Katy Christ, Fargo!" Lofley complained. "These son-of-a-bitchin' skeeters are eatin' us alive! At least free our hands, uh?"

Fargo didn't care a frog's fat ass what mosquitoes did to those two compost heaps. However, Lindy and Newt, too, were suffering miserably, as was Fargo. Each slap left a blood splotch on his exposed skin, in turn luring more of the pests. The air inside the cavern was blurred from their numbers, and they were no longer a mere nuisance—Fargo had heard of mosquitoes driving cattle *and* human beings mad.

"I'll be right back," he told Newt and Lindy, both busy slapping at the maddening pests. "Help's on the way."

Fargo strapped on his heavy leather gun belt, then drew the Colt and palmed the wheel to check the loads. He stepped out into the predawn darkness, eyes carefully scanning to all sides. He could hear the flood water coursing along the trail below, but with much less force. Fargo guessed it would recede by sunrise.

There was a dark red berry Fargo didn't know the name of, but Indians had shown him how its juice would keep off mosquitoes for hours. It grew widely on bushes in the mountains. Using his hat as a basket, he picked plump clusters of the berry, never forgetting to keep vigilant eyes in motion.

Above him on the mountain slope there was a brief rustling noise. In a heartbeat Fargo's Colt leaped into his fist. He thumbed the hammer back, carefully watching the moonlit trees. Fargo heard the soft rhythm of rain dripping in the leaves, but nothing else.

More rustling, closer this time, and Fargo began taking up the trigger slack. A moment later a foraging raccoon raced past him, and Fargo felt a grin of relief tugging at his lips.

"Son," he told himself as he turned back to the bushes, "you're turning into a nervous Nellie."

Thunk. Thunk.

Fargo flinched when two objects suddenly dropped into the wet leaves near his feet. The moment he saw sparks flying, his blood seemed to stop and flow backward in his veins—two sticks of dynamite were on the verge of turning him into stew meat!

Fargo hadn't survived for so long by freezing up at critical moments. Defusing would take longer than disposal. Heart in his throat, he speared the first stick of dynamite and heaved it back up the slope with all his might. Immediately he pounced on the second stick and flipped it away, too.

The first flood of relief was just washing over him when Fargo heard a heart-sickening sound: the impact when the second stick collided with an overhead branch. The moment it bounced in front of him for a second time, Fargo knew it was too late. He cursed and did a backward flip down the slope.

There was a fiery, sulfurous blast like the last ding-dong of doom, and Fargo felt something hard crash into his skull like a mule kick before his world closed down to blackness and silence.

12

"Bring the meddling bastard around first, Lumpy. I ain't about to waste Judge Lash on no unconscious man."

Fargo, his head throbbing like a giant abscess, heard the words only faintly, like a voice through a closed door. Water splashed into his face, but he kept his eyes closed, trying to get his derailed thoughts back on track.

"Is this the best time, Jack?" asked a second voice, tinny with nervousness. "I thought our first target was the skirt?"

"No better time than now, Lumpy. Wagner was dead wrong—it's Fargo we need to kill first. With him cold as a wagon wheel, who or what can stop us from walking into that cave and killing the rest? That apple-cheeked little priss she calls her brother?"

"All that rings right, Jack. What I mean is—*killing* Fargo, sure. But is this the best time to whip him?"

"It is unless you want to wet nurse the lanky crusader on the trail. I told you that son of a bitch would taste the cowhide before I hack his head off. Once I've had my pleasure with the whip, we'll toss a shot into his heart to finish him. Then we'll decapitate him and toss the head in a gunnysack. Before we leave, we'll spring Coyote and Stone and kill the other two."

"Yeah, but I still think—"

"Shut your piehole," Slade snapped. "You already talked me into using the dynamite before we should've. I'm the ramrod here, and I say Fargo *will* taste the cowhide."

By now Fargo had regained enough awareness to realize he was in one of the roughest scrapes of his life. "Jack" had to be Terrible Jack Slade, wanted for more than a

125

dozen murders in the South Pass country of Wyoming. His cruelly altered whip was the terror of San Francisco.

More water slapped into Fargo's face. He kept his eyes closed, buying time—but for what?

"C'mon, you sanctimonious bastard," Slade's gravelly voice said again. "You ain't hurt that bad."

Whatever blast debris had struck Fargo in the right temple had left him with a vicious headache. He was lashed to a large tree, its rough bark pressing into his forehead. All trussed up for a vicious beating, and the moment Fargo blacked out Slade meant to snuff his wick.

"You're faking, Fargo," Slade's voice snarled. "Maybe *this* will get a rise out of you."

A piercing whistle, when Slade's whip cut through the air, was followed by the earsplitting crack as the deadly popper ripped open Fargo's buckskin shirt. He had to bite his bottom lip until it bled, so painful was the damage caused by that brutally modified popper.

"Sure as shit he's awake," Slade gloated. "He wouldn't flinch that hard if he wasn't. S'matter, Fargo? Big, bad Trailsman can't take the terror of meeting Jack Slade?"

"Untie this rope," Fargo invited, face twisted with pain, "and I'll meet you proper—face to face."

Harsh, mocking laughter was followed by the singing whistle of the whip. Fire razored a line across Fargo's back, and he felt a sharp, jagged piece of stone rip its way loose when Slade pulled the whip back. The sadistic killer followed on with a half dozen more lashes.

"How do you like being a buttinsky *now*, Fargo?" Slade taunted him. "It's only got started, you overrated squaw man. I'm gonna peel your back like a flayed hog."

A piercing whistle, a vicious cracking sound, and this time Fargo could not help an involuntary grunt when pain too terrible to measure set his back ablaze. Blood coursed down it in rivulets, and he could feel lacerations deep enough to expose red meat.

Come on, Newt, Fargo prayed. *You're the only hope of rescue.* He didn't know how far away the cave was now, and Newt had not been very effective on the trail—in fact, had not hit one damn target he'd aimed at. Still, even a long shot was better than no chance at all.

"Escort *this,* Fargo," Slade snarled just before delivering a blow so fierce Fargo felt he'd been cut in half. When Slade snapped the whip back, embedded flint and obsidian felt like fishhooks ripping free.

Fargo had just been knocked out by the dynamite blast. Now, as blow after blow rained bloody hell on his back and shoulders, he saw darkness ebbing at the edge of his vision. He realized with desperate clarity—his only chance was to buy time by remaining conscious and deliberately prolonging the brutal beating. The moment he succumbed to the blessed oblivion of unconsciousness, Slade had other plans: *we'll decapitate him and toss the head in a gunnysack.*

"Had enough, law licker?" Slade demanded, his breath whistling in his nostrils from exertion.

In fact Fargo had had *too* much. After at least a dozen blows his back felt cut by a thousand knives, and so much meat and muscle were exposed that even a simple breeze felt excruciating.

"Tell you the straight," he replied through gritted teeth, "I can't feel it—same thing the whores tell you when you stick that tiny tallywhacker of yours inside them."

Fargo, awash on a red sea of pain, heard the man called Lumpy snigger. "Sorry, Jack. But that ballsy bastard is funny."

"Is he?" Slade said with ominous foreboding. "Then by all means, let's give him more of the tiny tallywhacker."

Fargo knew he was taking a desperate gamble by provoking Slade to continue the beating in a bid for time. When at least six more powerful blows lacerated his back, almost without pause between them, he feared he would lose his gamble as overwhelming pain forced him to black out. He barely clung to consciousness like a drowning man hanging on to a log.

"Shit, he's been whipped sick and silly," Lumpy said impatiently. "Look, the cockchafer can barely hold his head up. Le'me toss some lead into him."

"Yeah, go ahead," Slade decided, sounding satisfied at last. He was also breathing hard from his exertions. "Skye Fargo finally had the sass whipped outta him. We'll get his head, then take care of business in that cave."

Damn it, Newt, Fargo thought. *I know you're not a coward, boy. Step into this!*

Fargo heard a handgun being cocked. Despite the hot,

throbbing, knife-edge pain burning like a grease fire all over his back, he found his voice again.

"You can take my head, Slade," he retorted. "But you'll never whip the sass out of me. You ain't man enough."

Fargo could tell, from the sudden silence, that both men were impressed. No victim of Judge Lash had ever begged for more.

"Fargo," Slade said, moving into position again behind his captive, "you've got a set on you. I'll give you that. But you ain't got the brains God gave a pissant. I will not abide any man who questions my manhood. You could've got a bullet to end your suffering. Now it'll be the whip that snuffs your light."

Fargo doubted he could survive many more of these punishing blows. He had already lost a significant quantity of blood. As he heard Slade suck in a big breath of air, prior to his next cut with Judge Lash, Fargo willed himself to remain stoic and strong.

Bwam!

The powerful roar of a huge-bore gun echoed off into the mountain darkness like a clap of thunder. A fist-sized chuck of tree, only a foot above Fargo's head, went flying off into the grainy darkness. Almost immediately after, a repeating rifle opened up, peppering the area with hornet-buzzing slugs.

Fargo expected the murdering trash to kill him before they fled. At the first sound of gunfire, however, they panicked.

"Back to the horses!" Slade yelled. "Sounds like militia troops!"

Fargo heard both men take off like scalded dogs, crashing back up the slope. A moment later he blacked out for the second time.

For uncounted minutes and hours Skye Fargo dreamt of fire, the pure hellfire of extreme pain. His body felt like one exposed, giant wound into which someone had packed salt. Even the simple act of breathing hurt.

Then, slowly, things began to change. The fire in his back began to cool, and even transform itself into a gentle, caressing, even sensuous pleasure.

Fargo's eyes eased open. Bright sunshine washed through

128

the cavern entrance. He was lying on his stomach, shirtless, and Lindy's was the first face he spotted. She gave him a quick and uncertain smile.

"Does it hurt, Skye?" she greeted him.

"Something fierce," he admitted. "Although it's easing now thanks to whatever you've done."

"First I washed your back good. Then I shook powdered alum into the cuts. After that I wrapped your back good in gauze soaked in gentian so the bandages won't stick."

Fargo was impressed. Wincing at the pain, he sat up gingerly. "Sounds like you know what you're doing."

"Lindy's a good nurse," Newt put in proudly. "She worked for a doctor back in Troy Grove. The hard part was getting you here after we untied you. Good thing you were able to stumble a little because we couldn't have carried you."

Fargo met the kid's eyes. "And *you* . . . you might be green, but you've got starch in your collar. You fired off the Sharps we took from Robles, didn't you? Then you opened up with the Volcanic?"

Newt looked chagrined. "Yeah. Criminy, Skye, I didn't mean to almost hit you. I just thought I'd scare those two men."

"Well, you still can't hit the broad side of a barn. But they saw it, all right, when you damn near knocked my tree in two. Maybe they figured field artillery was aimed at them. Anyhow, they rabbited without even remembering to kill me. Thanks, Newt."

"I'd've been out there sooner," Newt admitted, "but those two explosions spooked us. Sounded like dynamite."

Fargo nodded. "It was. One stick damn near went off in my face."

"Must not have," Coyote chimed in. "You're still ugly as proud flesh."

"Dynamite, hey?" Lofley piped up. "Why, that sounds dangerous, Fargo. This trip could be bad for your sweetheart's health. Let me take you directly to Wagner and all your troubles are over."

"It's past peace piping," Fargo assured both killers. "And you two ain't calling the shots, so clam up before I kick your goddamn, furry teeth out."

"Who were those guys out on the slope, Skye?" Newt

asked. "Even in the dark, the one swinging the whip looked demented."

A dark cloud moved across Fargo's crop-bearded face. Seeing the promise of death in that look, Newt and Lindy exchanged quick glances.

"That hombre is Terrible Jack Slade," Fargo replied, "head of the San Francisco Vigilante Committee. 'Demented' is a good word for him. Me and him *will* be huggin'."

Newt asked, "How 'bout the second one? Who's he?"

"That's got me treed," Fargo admitted.

He glanced again at the two prisoners, both watching him with cunning expressions.

"The other one I don't know," Fargo said. "Didn't see his face, either. But his name is Lumpy. I'd bet my horse you two know him."

"Why, Fargo!" Coyote tried to look offended, but ended up smirking. "Me 'n' Stone here, why, we're missionaries for baby Jesus."

"Here's a safety tip, Fargo," Lofley added. "Don't *even* lock horns with Slade or Lumpy. You fancy yourself quite the struttin' rooster, but *them* old boys will turn you into a capon."

"They just had their chance," Fargo said. "And I'm still a rooster."

"Yeah, because a snot-nosed punk who don't know his ass from his elbow pulled your bacon outta the fire, big man. Do you hide behind babies, too?"

Newt scowled. "Untie that filthy goat, Skye. I'll show him how snot-nosed I am."

Lofley, however, remembered quite well how the young lumberjack had bounced Joaquin Robles—a huge, strong man—around like a child's ball down near San Bernardino.

"Ease off, kid," Lofley said. "I got no kick with you."

Newt stood his ground. "You can insult Skye all you like, he can take care of himself. But you keep insulting my sister and *I'll* have a kick with you."

Fargo, in evident pain, stood up. The buckskin shirt Lindy had literally pried off his back lay beside his blanket, shredded past any use as a shirt. He pulled his only extra from a saddlebag.

"What's it like outside?" he asked Newt. "Any standing water?"

"While you were out cold I used your hold ropes and went down to the trail. Nothing but some deep puddles. And, of course, mud."

Fargo nodded. "In this hot sun, that mud's drying out right now. By the time we scare up a little grub, and get the wagon back down to the trail, things'll be dry enough to head north."

Lindy looked emotionally torn. "Skye, your back has been deeply and repeatedly lacerated. Can you ride?"

"Do you still need to reach San Francisco by November first?"

"More than ever," she assured him.

"Then I can ride," Fargo told her. "There's two pretty ladies counting on me."

Lindy's face became a mask of puzzlement. "Two?"

"Sure. You and your sister."

A tear sprang to Lindy's eye, but her face glowed with joy.

"Didja prong the sister too, Fargo, you sly dog?" Coyote barbed. "With twins, are they ig-zacly alike—unh!"

Newt, whose throwing arm was exceptional, wasn't about to let these mange pots sully his sisters. With a quiet curse he grabbed a pebbly handful of heavy mud from outside the cavern entrance and sailed it hard into Coyote's face. He loosed a yelp when it smacked him, rocking his head back.

"Skye's in charge here, mister," Newt fumed. "But like I just warned you: when my sisters are insulted, it's my responsibility. The next one of you who mentions either one of them, I'm throwing a rock, not mud."

Fargo grinned while Coyote spat mud out of his mouth. His lips were pockmarked with small cuts.

"You heard the lad, boys," Fargo said. "Best launder your talk."

"Your *lad* is gonna regret that," Coyote said in a flat, deadly tone.

"His conscience is clean," Fargo assured the Apache. "*You're* the hellbound bastard. I guarantee it, Messy. Not only will I deliver you to law, but I'll be grinning from the crowd when you swing."

"Big boy like you, Fargo," Coyote said before he closed his eyes, "needing a sugar tit called justice. It's all a rich man's lie—you don't see that?"

"The law is flawed, all right," Fargo conceded. "But it's good enough to hang you."

Fargo noticed it again: Stone Lofley, aware of Lindy's close proximity, had not joined in this coarse sexual teasing and was avoiding her eyes—just as she was avoiding his.

"You're a lawyer, Beau," Prescott Wagner said. "You know how it works. 'Truth' is just putting on its boots while a lie travels halfway around the world. I'm telling you we *can* control this thing. Tom Trumble is just another crusader with his head up his ass."

Attorney Beau Garrett stared at his client across an immaculate desk of heavy, expensive teak—a desk Wagner's money had purchased. Garrett was courtly and gaunt with silvering hair. Early in the morning fog was almost always on the hills and mountains surrounding much of San Francisco, and Wagner could see it now through the big bay window of Garrett's Monterey Street office.

"You underrate Trumble," the lawyer replied, his face troubled. "The man is a formidable prosecutor. He actually sued the state of Illinois on behalf of Mormon plaintiffs and won the case. I was under the impression we wouldn't be going to court because of . . . an accident that might involve Trumble."

"Yeah, I was under that impression, too," Wagner admitted. "But the security around him has been excellent."

"And, evidently, the security around Malinda Helzer has been excellent, too," Garrett pointed out in his sonorous courtroom voice. "Which means there's an excellent chance she will indeed spill the beans on November first. If she does, we're both ruined."

Despite the early hour, Wagner was sipping another beloved julep from his buffalo-horn cup. Each time he raised the cup to his lips, his coat sleeves slid back to reveal the genuine pearl snaps on his cuffs.

"She can't spill *any* beans if she's dead," Wagner reminded his counsel. "And there's still many miles of dangerous trail before she gets here."

Garrett looked pained. "Prescott, we've gone round and

round on this before. Don't give me details. I'm an attorney, not your partner."

Wagner's florid face hardened. "The hell's got into you—religion?"

An American flag, in a standard behind Garrett's desk, was meant to convey his pro-Union, law-abiding values. However, he had encountered "certain difficulties," as he put it, while practicing law back in Baton Rouge, Louisiana. Some damning allegations were made by a neighbor's eleven-year-old daughter. Until, that is, his longtime acquaintance Wagner arranged for a "carriage accident" that killed the girl's father and served to scare the mother and daughter into silence forever. However, certain rumors persisted, and Garrett accompanied Wagner out west as his personal lawyer.

"Religion is nothing to the matter," Garrett finally replied. "It's just that I don't live in your pocket, Prescott."

"Oh?" Wagner, comfortably sprawled on a leather sofa, looked amused. "Then you don't *live,* do you?"

Garrett looked miserable and trapped, but Wagner hadn't one jot of sympathy for the hapless fool. Money, Wagner figured, was like manure—it worked best when it was spread around. He had spread plenty around San Francisco, including to Garrett, and now it was time for the harvest.

"Beau, let me give it to you candidly. You're a Harvard graduate from a genteel family. I'm the son of a bootlegger who sold whiskey to warring Indians. Your people, and you yourself, consider me one of the new pick-and-shovel millionaires. Plenty of money, but no manners to go with it. Well, *I'm* the future of California, and this"—he swept out an arm to indicate the entire city—"is *my* empire, not Mrs. Astor's. Once we win this case, and I win the mayoral election, then we—*we,* Beau, because you're the legal genius—will control the township charter."

Garrett shook his head. "Win the case? That's easy if Malinda Helzer doesn't show up in time. Tom Trumble is new out here, still seen as an outside meddler. While he does have some strong evidence against you, in the form of illegally filed claims, he doesn't realize how hard it is to bring convictions out west. The jury will never prosecute you for the stated charges."

Wagner looked smug. "No, because I'm widely seen as 'harum-scarum.' Reckless, but not seriously criminal. Reckless is admired out West."

"True, but rape is not. If the woman takes the stand, all bets are off."

Despite Wagner's devil-may-care manner, he fully concurred with this last point. "I haven't heard a word from Jack Slade," he admitted. "But he hasn't been gone that long. If another day passes without hearing from him and Lumpy, it'll be growing more likely that Fargo has sent them to eternity. In which case it'll be up to the boys here in town to take care of business."

Garrett didn't look too reassured. "From what I've heard about him, Skye Fargo would ride into hell with a pocketful of firecrackers."

"He's worth respecting," Wagner agreed. "But don't forget—an 'accidental' fire could take down the courthouse and all its vulnerable records. For that matter, even during the trial some drunken fool might toss dynamite through a window, dynamite that just happens to land near the prosecution table. Trumble *and* the woman, up in one flash before she can sing."

Garrett paled. "If that drunken fool rolls it twenty feet too far, the defense table goes up. I prefer the fire idea."

Wagner laughed. "If that man is neither drunk nor a fool, he'll land it accurately. Just bear in mind—Jack Slade and Lumpy are good field operatives and may well be alive yet. If so, the Old Mission Trail remains very much a death trap for Fargo and the Helzer woman."

Lowering the wagon down to the trail was much easier than raising it had been. Only the occasional patch of mud, and widely scattered debris, proved there had even been a powerful flash flood the night before.

Thanks to Lindy's excellent repair job on him, Fargo wasn't suffering too much pain from the savage whipping. The pace they held—a slow trot so the prisoners could keep it up without many pauses—eased Fargo's pain. Even so, each time the Ovaro's hooves hit an uneven spot in the trail, pain jolted across Fargo's whip-ravaged back.

"You gonna settle up with that Terrible Jack Slade, Skye?" Newt asked about two hours into that day's trek.

He drove the team, Lindy seated on a pallet of blankets in the wagon bed.

"It's no vendetta," Fargo replied, eyes scanning the slopes. "But if my trail crosses his, I mean to square the balance."

"Kill him? I would."

"Newt!" Lindy snapped. "Leave Skye alone. You're being ghoulish!"

Laughing at her prim tone, Fargo pulled down his hat against the swirling dust—a good sign the drying out was complete. He winced when his hat scraped the tender knot over his right temple.

On their left the ocean was screened from view by tall bushes. Fresh water was temporarily scarce, so when Fargo spotted an old streambed they reined in. He dug into the bed for seepage, filling canteens first and then letting the horses drink.

"Skye? May I ride with you for just a short distance?" Lindy asked. "I mean, with you on your horse?"

Fargo looked surprised. "Lady, I welcome your company, believe me. But you can prob'ly imagine the kind of sewer filth those two prisoners will spew. They know Newt's under strict orders not to stop, so they don't fear his wrath. Not to mention that riding double's not the best thing for my horse."

"Just a few minutes would be long enough. There's something I want to tell you, and I don't want those nosy jackals listening in."

"Can't it wait until we camp tonight?" Fargo suggested.

"Maybe it could, but I might chicken out by then."

Fargo's strong white teeth flashed through his beard when he laughed. "Now you got me curious."

Fargo patted the Ovaro's neck as warning, knowing the stallion didn't like to be surprised by a double load. Then he stepped up and over before reaching down to help Lindy up behind him.

"Press close against me," he urged in a sly tone. "Case Indians attack, of course."

"That's pure bosh," she said, laughing right back. "But I'll be happy to press close. Like this?"

"There goes *your* spot in heaven," he teased as the touch of her ample charms forced him to adjust himself. When the wagon was well ahead of them, Fargo said, "All right, woman of mystery—what's all this hugger-mugger about?"

"No hugger-mugger. It's just . . . you've done so much for me, *suffered* so much for me. And you mentioned once that you think what I'm doing is important. Oh, it *is*, Skye, so very important. I want you to know the truth, and besides, you've guessed much of it anyway."

Fargo listened attentively, but also kept his hawk eyes in motion. The next attack could come at any moment, and Fargo wasn't about to forget the near success of the last.

"This isn't my first trip out West," Lindy admitted. "Three years ago next month, my sister and I went out to the Arizona Territory to live with our uncle Frank. He had made a fortune in silver mining and always doted on us. At the time Belinda was newly widowed and three months pregnant."

"Hey, Fargo!" Coyote shouted from ahead. "Skip the sweet talk and strip her buck!"

"His comeuppance will arrive soon," Fargo told Lindy. "Go ahead."

"Well . . . a human monster named Prescott Wagner was also out there at the time. Something about buying up claims to consolidate ownership."

"Fancy name for stealing, but go ahead."

"He showed up at my uncle's house, drunk and brutish in his behavior. We told him my uncle was gone to a miners' meeting, but he was instantly smitten by Belinda—in the animal sense, not the romantic. Why her and not me I'll never know. He repeatedly raped her, then killed her with a knife—so brutally that organs were released."

"Stone Lofley figures into the mix too, right?" Fargo prompted when she fell silent.

"Yes, you're absolutely right that I've been avoiding his eyes. He stood guard over me outside and killed my uncle Frank when he came home. Then he shot me and left me for dead. But the shot was poorly aimed, only grazed my side. I collapsed as if dead."

Fargo nodded. "Just curious. Makes perfect sense that you wouldn't want to look at Lofley. But *he* ain't got no fine feelings, so why is he avoiding looking at you? Few men under eighty could pull that off."

As the woman pressed snugly against him hesitated, all curves and firm bulges, Fargo could almost feel her blushing.

"Because," she replied, "he tried several times to rape me and failed. He . . . even cried once. I think he's ashamed that I'm alive and know his secret."

"Oh, Jesus," Fargo muttered, "one of those."

For a moment he recalled the terrifying arsonist Blaze Weston, whom he battled in the New Mexico Territory. He, too, could not perform with the ladies, and many innocent lives were sacrificed as a result.

"I'll personally see him hang," Fargo promised. "My only question is how you finally ended up going to San Francisco. Did you get word Wagner was there?"

"Not exactly. I learned, from an Associated Press story in the newspapers, that officials in San Francisco wanted to try Wagner on several serious charges. It's an important test case to see if law and order can be established out here. But they lacked any willing witness as to his character. So I wired a Tom Trumble, and he sent me some money to cover expenses."

"Well, there it is," Fargo said thoughtfully. "You're right. I put most of it together. Except the part about November first being a test case. This is going to be mighty damn important, Lindy. Important for you, for San Francisco, hell, for the entire West. You're a mighty brave gal—as brave as you are pretty."

"Hey, Fargo!" Coyote hollered again. "Ain't that white squaw at least givin' you a reach-around?"

"Yessir," Fargo repeated, his eyes narrowing, "mighty damn important."

13

By day's end Fargo's group had drawn within sight of La Purisima Mission. It stood on a point jutting out to sea, quiet and dark in the fading daylight—even sinister as shadows enveloped it.

"Just like I figured," Fargo remarked to Newt and Lindy. "It's no longer being used by the church. There's well-built missions all up and down the coast, some of 'em deserted like this one. Mighty handy for all the road gangs."

The three of them stood on the shore of a rocky cove. To their left, the shimmering green Pacific now looked like calm, dark glass as the bloodred sun prepared to plunge beneath the horizon. They had pitched a simple camp at the head of the cove, where the prisoners were securely tied to trees.

"Road gangs?" Lindy repeated. "You suspect Slade and his partner are staying there?"

"I'd back good odds, yeah. They did a fair job of covering their tracks, but I found sign of them all day. Headed right here."

"The mission's only about a half mile farther north," Newt pointed out. "Want to see if the tracks turn in there?"

Fargo shook his head, watching sea water dash to foam on the craggy rocks. "Proving that is less important than staying out of sight. They'll be there, all right."

"How can you be so certain of that?" Lindy asked.

"Because a killer, even the rare smart one, is predictable," Fargo replied. "La Purisima is perfect for ambushing anyone on this trail. On the west, it's prac'ly falling into the ocean. On the east are steep sand dunes you can't see from here. So the trail is forced to narrow, and it's less than ten feet from *that*."

Fargo pointed to the mission belfry at the southeast corner of the adobe building.

"It commands an excellent view of the trail," he explained. "Hell, even Deadeye Newt here could kill from up there. If I was a jobber hired to kill someone traveling on the coast, that place would be high on my list."

"So . . . how do we get by?" Lindy asked.

"We'll just spread our blankets here tonight. I need to rest my back, and besides, I want to scout that mission in daylight. We'll get by somehow," Fargo assured her.

They returned to the wagon, its tongue propped on a stone to avoid water damage from the still-damp earth.

" 'Preciate it, Newt, if you'd stand first watch," Fargo said over a plateful of bland beans. "Our friends, if they're holed up in the mission, won't likely leave it now. But I've spotted plenty of hoofprints along this section of the trail, and smart money says it ain't express riders. So stay alert and watch my stallion close. He'll give warning at any trouble."

"Hey, Fargo!" Coyote's rusty voice shouted as the Trailsman, walking gingerly, headed for his blankets. "Sleep tight and don't let the bedbugs bite!"

"Yeah, sweet dreams, hero!" Loflcy added. "Jack Slade and Lumpy just might be comin' to tuck you in. Permanent like."

"You boys seem to rate these two mighty high," Fargo remarked.

Coyote laughed. "So would you if you knew them. Fargo, you're already dead."

"Can't be, unless they serve beans in the afterlife."

Fargo used his Arkansas toothpick to soften the ground before he unrolled his blanket and canvas groundsheet. Eyes weighted with exhaustion, he willed himself to stay awake until he'd cleaned and oiled both his Colt and Henry. Then he laid them within easy reach and fell into a deep sleep almost immediately.

"Skye! *Psst*, Skye! Cripes, wake up!"

Still half asleep, Fargo reacted instinctively when a hand grabbed his shoulder. His right hand shot down to jerk the Arkansas toothpick from its boot sheath.

"Holy Toledo! Skye, it's me, Newt! Don't stab me."

Fargo came fully awake, wincing when he sat up fast. "The hell you doing, touching a sleeping man, Newt? Out West that'll get you buried."

"We might get buried anyway, Skye. Look—your pinto has alerted."

Newt was right. In the generous moonlight Fargo could see the Ovaro facing the trail, ears pricked, nose sampling the air.

"Seen or heard anything yet?" Fargo demanded, grabbing his Henry and levering a round into the chamber. He stood up, then knelt again to feel the ground with three fingertips.

"Doesn't work here," he fretted. "The damn ocean shakes the ground too much. I can't feel horses."

Even as Fargo finished speaking, a shadowed group of riders appeared out on the trail, approaching from the south. Fargo had no exact idea how many, but it was a formidable group—perhaps a dozen to fifteen.

"Our two friends again, back with reinforcements?" Newt asked in a whisper. He had crouched beside Fargo with his Volcanic repeating rifle in his right hand.

"Nope. It's a gang up from Mexico. I can see *tapaderos* instead of regular stirrups on their horses."

"Tapa-what?"

"Big wooden guards that cover the entire foot and ankle. They use 'em in spiny cactus country. We should be all right, Newt. They can't see our camp from the trail, and unless they're bothering to track us in darkness, there's no reason for them to—"

Just then one of the team horses whinnied loudly, and Fargo's heart sank as he realized—*now* the Mexican road bandits had an excellent reason to rein in.

"Shit," he said, dropping into a prone position and scooping out a hole for his left elbow. "Now we're up against it, Newt. They don't know how many of us there are, and we're not going to let them find out."

"How do we pull that off—magic?" Newt didn't sound too convinced.

"Won't need magic. We've both got fast repeaters and forty-six rifle rounds between us without reloading. Our only chance is to come right out of the chute bucking. We toss up a wall of lead, Newt. Just like you did when we busted out of Los Angeles."

The scared but plucky kid dug in beside Fargo. "All right, a wall of lead it is."

"Just remember that night fighting marks your location for the enemy each time the muzzle flashes. Roll to a new spot after every two or three shots. That'll also make it look like we got more men in the fight "

The riders had detoured in toward the beach. Fargo wasted no time.

"Put at 'em, Newt!" he urged, squeezing off his first round before any of the riders could swing down.

Newt was weak on accuracy, but adept at working a rifle smoothly. He opened fire right behind Fargo, an unrelenting burst that matched the Trailsman's Henry. Both men rolled to new positions just in time—the return fire from the Mexicans' guns sent lead whiffing in deadly profusion.

Gritting his teeth at the pain in his injured back, Fargo rolled across the beach, levering his Henry. He snapped off three more rounds, the rifle stock slapping his cheek. The road gang's bullets thumped into the dirt all around them. Some arced high and plinked into the ocean behind them.

Across the beach, red muzzle streaks marked the bandits' position. They were stupidly remaining clustered, and the surprise attack left them unsure whether to dismount and fight or simply get the hell out.

Sensing that one casualty might send them running, Fargo drew a bead on a muzzle streak, then raised the barrel a half inch and fired. A shrill cry of pain told him the bullet found its man.

"*Now,* Newt!" Fargo said. "The surprise hasn't wore off yet. If they overcome it, we're gone beavers. Make it *hot* for those chilipeps! We can haze 'em off with another good volley."

This was no time for caution. Fargo leading the way, both men charged the group under cover of darkness, spraying hot lead before them. Neither man worried about careful aiming, only rapid fire, shooting from the hip.

Another man cried out, cursing in Spanish. That broke

the bandits' will. Unsure what manner of demons had taken over the beach, one of them cried out, *"Vamanos, muchachos! De prisa!"*

Newt let loose a whoop. "It worked, Skye! We scared 'em off!"

Fargo, however, skipped any celebrating. He listened until he was sure the riders were indeed headed north again.

"Damn, Newt," he praised the tenderfoot, thumping his back so hard the kid almost fell down. "You got more guts than a smokehouse. It took a brave man to charge all those mounted bandits."

"Actually, I was mostly just scared," the youth confessed.

"It's the staying and doing that matters. 'Scared' doesn't mean coward. Hell, I'm scared plenty of times."

They went to check on Lindy, who was shaken but unharmed.

"My Lord, all that racket," she told Fargo. "It sounded like two armies were clashing."

"Yeah, that's right, innit? All that racket," Fargo repeated thoughtfully, gazing at the fortresslike silhouette La Purisima traced against a blue-black sky—especially the belfry.

"What's wrong, Skye?" Newt asked.

"Assuming Slade and his pal Lumpy are in that mission," Fargo replied, "which I'm mighty certain they are, there's no way in hell they could've missed this cartridge session. It doesn't *prove* we're nearby, of course. But they'd have to be even stupider than God made 'em if they don't at least suspect it."

Newt nodded, catching on. "Now you won't have the element of surprise when you visit that place tomorrow."

"You're learning battle tactics, old son. That's exactly what's wrong. Always surprise, mystify, and confuse your enemy—most fights go to the side that best uses surprise."

"If all that is true," Lindy fretted, "is it wise for you to ride up there?"

Fargo laughed. "*Wise?* Lady, the last wise thing I did was in picking out my horse. But the thing is—I have to go there. Those two murdering scuts have got rifles *and* dynamite. Rifles might miss, sure, but dynamite don't require such fine aiming. If we want to get past that mission, we're gonna hafta clean the rats out first."

Fargo rolled out just before sunrise. Newt was already awake, having stood the last stint of guard duty. The smell of strong coffee wafted to Fargo's nostrils.

"How's the back?" Newt greeted him, handing Fargo a cup of coffee.

"Sometimes it feels like a hot branding iron is being pressed into it," Fargo admitted. "It's better, though, since Lindy put the new bandage on it last night."

"Lindy's still asleep and so are the prisoners," Newt reported. "Man, we've still got a long way to haul those buzzards."

"We'll bring 'em to justice," Fargo said confidently. He remembered what Lindy had told him yesterday about Stone Lofley out in Arizona. "*Rope* justice," he added.

After gnawing on a little dried fruit and drinking plenty of water, Fargo whistled in the Ovaro and tacked him. With the scent of the sea in his nostrils, the stallion seemed more rambunctious than usual.

"Hooves look good, old warhorse," Fargo said, examining each in turn. "Sores are healed and no cracks."

By the time the stallion was trail ready, Lindy and the prisoners were all awake.

"Fargo, if horseshit was brains you'd have a clean corral," Coyote called out from his tree. "Ain't you never heard that saying, 'Poke not fire with a sword?' You go lookin' for Terrible Jack Slade, and mister, you're lookin' for your own grave."

"Nice to know you care about me, Coyote. But we *ain't* swappin' spit."

Coyote loosed a bray of laughter. "You're a hard man to kill, Trailsman. But every man's string has to run out. Yours runs out this morning."

"I've been pronounced dead plenty of times," Fargo replied calmly. "Either that was hokum or I've been resurrected from the dead a few dozen times."

"Yeah," Stone Lofley tossed in, "but that was before you tangled with Terrible Jack. I pity you, boy. Before this morning is over, you'll wish you'd died as a child."

Fargo tipped his hat. "I'll give Slade your regards."

Still afoot, and sticking to the tree cover curving along the cove, Fargo studied La Purisima in the still weak morning light. The trees blocked a full view, so he employed a scouting trick he often used on the open plains—he selected the tallest tree in the area and shinnied up, his back forcing him to move gingerly.

The view, from atop a sycamore tree, gave Fargo a better mind map of the mission. He understood immediately, when he saw a white towel tied to the wrought-iron gate, why the place was apparently no longer an Indian school— that towel was the universal warning that plague had infected a place. Which might have kept Slade and Lumpy from holing up there.

"That," Fargo muttered to himself, "or Slade tied it there himself to put me off my guard."

It bothered Fargo, this no longer being sure. His trail-trained eyes studied the location minutely, but there was little to see besides endless green ocean on its left flank, brush on its right—brush that wrapped around behind the mission.

Suddenly, just as Fargo's patient eyes studied the brush crowding the northeast corner of the mission, he saw what looked like a horse tail flick into view for a moment before disappearing again.

A grin tugged at Fargo's lips and he climbed quickly down. Nothing like a quick scout to tell a man where he stood.

"See anything?" Newt asked while Fargo booted his Henry and swung up onto the hurricane deck.

"All I needed to see, lumberjack. Keep a close eye on those two roaches."

"Skye, be careful!" Lindy called from the wagon, where she sat running a horn brush through her blond tresses.

"Careful? That there's a dead man on horseback, sweet britches!" Coyote cried out gleefully. "After he takes the dirt nap, you and baby brother are next. With buckskin boy dead, you're gonna need comfortin'—*ouch! Jee-zus Christ!*"

True to his earlier promise, Newt had tossed a stone at Coyote for insulting his sister. Luckily for Coyote it was small and only bruised the Apache's lips.

"Life gets a mite strange at times," Fargo remarked

philosophically as he rode north along the Old Mission Trail.

Fargo knew he couldn't approach the mission on horseback once the tree cover thinned out. When he reached the last of the screening timber, he led the Ovaro well off the trail and hobbled him. From there, keeping out of sight from the two open sides of the bell tower, he bent low and kept to the tall grass.

Confirming his hunch, he slipped around behind the big adobe structure and found two horses hidden there, a sorrel in reasonably good shape and a blood bay with vicious shoulder scars—proof positive it was an outlaw's horse.

"Easy goes it," Fargo calmed both nervous mounts. Their riders were so cruel and negligent they hadn't even stripped the leather before tethering their mounts. There was neither food nor water in sight.

Fargo stripped them now, loosened the tethers, and pointed the horses north, slapping them on their rumps. Not only did he intend to leave Slade and Lumpy horseless, but Fargo made it a policy to liberate outlaw horses when he could. They were almost always better off on their own.

Fargo recalled his trouble with cartridge failure down in the Mojave. He removed his Colt, opened the loading gate, and blew a quick puff of air into the works to dislodge blown sand. He gave the same treatment to his brass-framed Henry, then headed quickly toward the belfry. Fargo was gambling that the two dynamite-tossing killers were up there now, watching the trail closely for their intended victims.

Scaling the outside wall was easy thanks to vigas, supporting timbers that jutted out from the wall every two feet or so. Fargo was still about ten feet from the opening in the tower when he heard someone speak.

"—that ruckus last night don't mean squat," insisted the voice of Terrible Jack Slade. "We already knew Gonzales brought his gang up from Rosarito. From the sound of that battle last night, it wasn't Fargo's bunch shooting back. Two men couldn't bust caps that quick."

"Maybe," Lumpy's voice said doubtfully. "I don't trust that goddamn Fargo. For all we know, he could be here right now."

"Of course we don't trust him, muttonhead. That's why we're gonna plant the son of a bitch."

Fargo, by necessity, had put Jack Slade and his monstrous whip from his thoughts. Hearing the voice now, however, made Fargo's vision go red at the edges.

He hauled himself up higher and tossed his hat down as he neared the ledge of the north opening in the tower. Fargo slowly edged his head over—a man with a goiter on his neck, obviously Lumpy, crimped a paper and shook some tobacco into it. He wore two Colt Navy revolvers in tie-down holsters, and a double-ten express gun leaned against the wall nearby.

Jack Slade held an early model Hunt repeating rifle, the same weapon Fargo suspected of firing those bizarre exploding bullets. The dynamite in an oilskin pouch at Slade's feet was already equipped with fuses—short fuses. From where Slade stood, it was almost straight down to the trail.

However, it was Judge Lash whom Fargo gave the longest stare—the most notorious whip in the American West. Even now, the burning pulses in his back reminded Fargo of that whip's deadly potential.

"We shoulda killed him when we had him tied up," Lumpy Neck complained.

"Add 'should' to a nail," Slade growled, "and you'll have a nail."

"We *had* the bastard dead to rights," Lumpy Neck persisted.

"He dies today," Slade predicted. "Better late than never, huh? Then we light a shuck toward their campsite, kill the girl and her brother, and set Coyote and Lofley free."

"No need to kill the girl *right* away," Lumpy reminded him. "Been a coon's age since I had any poon."

Fargo knew damn good and well he wasn't about to add these two vicious hardcases to his string. So he decided to let them dig their own graves by their actions—he simply cleared his throat loudly behind them and waited.

Both men leaped like butt-shot dogs. When they spun around, they stared into the unblinking eye of Fargo's Colt.

"Don't get spooky on me, boys," Fargo advised, wagging the Colt's muzzle for emphasis. "Or it's curtains for both of you."

Fargo knew damn well they *would* get spooky, so he watched their hands, not their eyes—eyes didn't pull triggers. Sure enough, Lumpy Neck's right hand had begun to open and close as he nerved himself up.

"Do it and you're dog meat," Fargo warned again, knowing the advice was useless.

Lumpy Neck, a quick-draw artist, decided a Navy Colt was his best bet, not the nearby shotgun. He fell deftly to one side, catching Fargo by surprise with the well-practiced move, and opened fire. The two men traded desperate shots, Fargo realizing with a sinking feeling that Slade was now free to lunge for that damned scattergun, knowing there'd be no chance of missing him.

A bullet parted Fargo's hair, another burned his left ear as it grazed him. A third shot chunked into the ledge and sent adobe dust into his eyes. He knew Slade had the sawed-off now and was raising it with a triumphant shout, but Fargo willed himself calm and aimed for the killing shot.

His fifth bullet drilled Lumpy Neck through the heart, and he was dead before he hit the floor. Now, however, a deadly split-second-long contest began: Slade had only to swing the barrels up, Fargo to swing his Colt left.

Fargo won. The Colt jumped, and a neat hole appeared in Slade's forehead. His eyes lost their focus, rolled up in his head, and the man-monster plummeted over the ledge to the ground below. The hair-trigger shotgun went off when it dropped, but fortunately for Fargo the big iron bell took most of the pellets. Still, the tremendous racket left his eardrums ringing for several minutes.

Fargo hauled Lumpy's body to the south opening Slade had fallen through, then tossed it down to the trail below beside his dead comrade. Fargo climbed back down, using the vigas again. There was still one more detail to arrange before he returned to camp.

Lindy ran to meet him when Fargo reined in to the camp on the cove. "Skye, are you all right?"

Fargo saw both prisoners listening intently. Coyote and Lofley had stared at each other in obvious disappointment when they first spotted him.

"Glad you're in one piece," Newt greeted him. "Holy moly, Skye! Gunshots, shotgun blasts, even bells ringing! What happened? Did you kill 'em?"

Fargo shook his head as he swung down. "Don't ask, Newt. Coyote and Lofley weren't shitting anybody—Jack Slade and Lumpy are death to the devil. I'm lucky I got out of there alive."

"See?" Coyote chortled. "*See?* Fargo, it's best to test the water before you wade in. We warned you."

Even Lofley was feeling frisky enough to taunt Fargo. "See how it's gonna be, Fargo? You think you was lucky just now, wait until next time. Face it, hero. You ain't got the caliber to handle those two."

"You ain't makin' it to 'Frisco, neither," Coyote said. "Your best bet is to put in with us. Wagner will pay top wages to a handy stag like you."

"Well . . ." Fargo tried to look indecisive. "You boys do seem to know 'b' from a banjo. Maybe I *am* on a fool's errand."

When Lindy and Newt stared at him, aghast, Fargo sent them a complicit wink.

"*Now* you're whistlin'," Lofley approved. "You don't *even* want Jack Slade puttin' you in his sights. Hell, you've already tasted Judge Lash. You're a stout hombre, Fargo, I'm the first to say it. But Jack Slade wasn't born of woman—he's the meanest killer in the West. You need to nail your colors to Wagner's mast, Fargo, and there'll be no more hog and hominy on your plate."

"Undo these ropes, pard," Coyote added.

"Maybe later," Fargo said evasively. "Let's get moving while I con things over."

La Purisima was only a half mile up the trail. As they first set out, both owlhoots continued their wheedling, trying to convince Fargo to spring them on the spot. As they drew nearer the mission, however, the two prisoners fell silent, trying to puzzle out what they were seeing ahead.

"What the hell?" Coyote said before lapsing into uneasy silence again.

Two men were resting lazily against the buttressed wall of the mission. One had a cigarette stuck into one corner of his mouth, the other had two sticks of dynamite protruding from a pocket.

Fargo's ears, trained on the open plains, picked it up when Lofley whispered to Coyote. "Christ sakes, that's

Slade and Lumpy just standin' in the open. They gone loco? Where's their weapons?"

Coyote not only had better eyes than Lofley, he was smarter. His face took on an ashen pallor. "Look closer, you clodpole. Fargo killed 'em both."

"That's about the size of it," Fargo snapped at the two shocked owlhoots. "The 'meanest killer in the West' is carrion bait, boys. But guess who lives on?"

Fargo reached into a saddlebag and pulled his little surprise out into plain view.

"Judge Lash," Coyote said, his voice almost giving out as Fargo uncoiled the infamous blacksnake whip.

"Yep, that's right. Judge Lash." Fargo gave it an expert snap, the deadly popper cracking loudly just over their heads. "You two are now being served official notice. At the first disrespectful comment that comes out of either one of your filthy sewers, you're *both* getting what Slade gave me. Is that clear?"

"Yes, sir," Coyote said.

"Yes, sir, Mr. Fargo," Lofley added quickly.

"That's more like it," Fargo said as he coiled Judge Lash again. "I'm a lovable cuss, and I'd just as soon get along with you fellows until we can get you hanged in proper style."

14

With Slade and Lumpy Neck dead, Fargo's group encountered no more serious difficulties for the rest of the journey. Fargo considered both of the dead bodies, especially Slade's, as potential evidence in Wagner's trial. There was an undertaker's parlor in San Luis Obispo, which meant the bodies could be preserved for short duration.

"I still don't get it," Newt said after Fargo explained why they were bothering to lug two corpses more than thirty miles. "What good are the bodies?"

"There's three witnesses here that somebody fired specially rigged exploding bullets at us, and especially at Lindy. I'll guarantee you that Jack Slade bragged up the invention of those bullets all over San Francisco. I can also prove I killed him by producing those bodies, my bullets still in them. The point is that Slade worked for Wagner and was doing his bidding."

Fargo left the bodies to a salt chest in San Luis Obispo. He had come to share Lindy's urgency, and Fargo ordered a quicker pace. With their prisoners sulky but cooperative, they reached Half Moon Bay, just south of San Francisco, on the morning of October 30—only two days before Wagner's trial began.

"I'm not too impressed, so far," Lindy admitted, gazing around. "All the hills in sight look like plucked chickens."

"They're taking all the available trees to timber mines," Newt told his sister.

Fargo rode his Ovaro to the right of the wagon. The trail had ended at Santa Cruz mission, and since then they'd followed the federal freight road, a deeply rutted, uncomfortable passage. Fargo had not relaxed his vigilance, and grew even more observant as they neared the most dangerous city in 1850s America.

"These boomtowns are always ugly at first," he remarked. "The main reason for being there is to make money. Once the families settle in you get schools, churches, and somebody starts talkin' up gaslights, sidewalks, and pretty parks. And law enforcement—the one thing Prescott Wagner and his ilk won't abide."

They rounded the shoulder of a bald hill, and Fargo pointed toward a tightly packed cluster of buildings—some brick, some new slab lumber—perched on a sheltered cove of the bay.

"How you like the view now, Lindy?" he asked.

"Not much better, I'm afraid. The setting should be beautiful, but these hills look so forlorn."

"The lack of pretty scenery won't be our biggest problem," Fargo suggested. "Both of you need to keep in mind that Wagner ain't a lone renegade. Sure, law is *trying* to be born in San Francisco or Lindy wouldn't be here. Right now, though, real law is just a pup—and it's the full-grown Hounds who still swagger it around. Lindy, especially, needs to lay low, avoid going out in public."

"You think Wagner would actually have her murdered right here in the city?" Newt asked.

"Oh, hell yes. I got no idea what kind of evidence this Tom Trumble fellow is sittin' on, but in a boomtown like this, convictions of rich men are rare—except for rapists and woman killers. They could sentence him to hang, using his crimes here in California as an excuse since they got no jurisdiction over what happened in Arizona Territory. Believe me, Wagner has to know all that."

Traffic on the freight road increased dramatically as they neared the chaotic city. Occasional gunshots rang out above the din of crowd noise and the bands making raucous music in the Barbary Coast tenderloin. Lindy and Newt stared in amazement at the flyblown shanties and tar-paper shacks on the outskirts of town, the Chinese and Mexican sectors.

"Oh, great," Newt muttered. "This up ahead looks like our first reception committee."

Fargo had already spotted him. The man had been standing in the muddy shoulder of the street, watching traffic closely. When he spotted the wagon he stepped abruptly out in front of them, raising his right hand to halt them.

"Typical example of the vermin hereabouts," Fargo told his companions. "Greasy clothes, gimlet eyes, stolen guns and a tin badge with no law whatsoever behind it. Best way to let 'em know we're here is to make a strong first impression."

"Whoa there!" Wagner's thug shouted as if he had a right to. Newt drew back on the reins.

The vigilante puffed himself up as he strolled around the wagon. Although he said nothing to Coyote and Lofley, Fargo could tell they all knew each other by the way they carefully avoided eye contact.

"Hope you folks ain't got no plans to roost here," he said, looking up at Fargo. "Nor even to stop long."

"Nah. *You* folks wouldn't want me," Fargo replied. "For a fact you wouldn't."

The man's turtle eyes narrowed even more. "And just why's that, mister?"

"I'm one helluva bully," Fargo announced proudly, his lake water eyes as direct as searchlights. "Terrible bully, matter fact. Don't like tin badges."

The vigilante had a stout build and wore a Smith and Wesson over each hip. Like most bullyboys, however, he was used to dishing it out, not taking it. After a surprised pause, he puffed himself back up again. "Oh, so you're about half rough, is that it?"

"*Double* rough don't even cover it," Fargo said, eyes still boring into the thug's. "Now me, I like to whip a tin-badge man until he begs for mercy. Then I top his woman right in front of him before I drag-hang him behind a slow horse."

A scarlet flush of anger flooded into the thug's face, but Fargo's unexpected and brutal talk had also set him back on his heels.

"Mister, you got brass," he said. "I'll give you that. But there ain't no cause for such tall talk."

"Even less cause for actually doing such things, right? That's why you two-bit bullyboys got two problems. One, *real* law is coming to San Francisco soon, and two, Skye Fargo is here *now*."

Obviously, Wagner did not tell all of his toadies that the

Trailsman would be escorting Lindy. This fellow before Fargo paled to a fish-belly white.

Fargo palmed his Colt and flicked off the riding thong. The vigilante's lower lip began to tremble.

"Wanna please your murdering boss?" Fargo asked. "Have a try at killing the woman."

The thug shook his head, backing away. "Kill the?—Mister, you're stark, staring crazy."

"Goddamn right I am," Fargo assured him. "And I get even crazier when men try to shoot an innocent woman. You spread the word, chawbacon—Prescott Wagner is finished."

The rodent scampered off to do just that. However, he found the courage to turn back around. "You're picking the wrong hill to die on, Fargo. Best leave now and take your friends with you."

As they started toward town proper, Fargo suggested they stay at the Crystal Palace Hotel on Alcalde Street. When they hit town, Newt cursed in dismay. Not only was traffic heavy, but the muddy streets were obviously being used as the town dump. Fargo spotted everything from dead animals to broken stoves—and he glimpsed a leather boot that seemed to have a foot in it.

"My lands, what is that smell?" Lindy gasped, holding a handkerchief over her nose.

"Better not to know," Fargo advised, thinking of that boot.

Fargo made their first stop the Plaza, the old central square, where he was gratified to find a U.S. deputy marshal and a small jailhouse. Newt and Lindy swore out a complaint. Drawings on the wanted dodger in Fargo's pocket were convincing enough to get Coyote and Stone Lofley locked up.

As Fargo, Lindy and Newt headed toward the Crystal Palace, Fargo noted that some things were improving in San Francisco. The saloon-set vigilantes no longer lorded it over the entire city, but were restricted to the waterfront, Telegraph Hill, and a few other spots. Fargo even noticed a few city roundsmen, in blue helmets, wearing official stars and behaving more decently.

"Still a hellhole," he remarked to the others. "But I see signs there'll be a civilized settlement here someday."

"Heck, maybe even a great one," Newt suggested, "given

this key location with prime access to both the ocean and the inland rivers."

"Trial's day after tomorrow," Fargo said, glancing down at a nervous-looking Lindy. "You got Trumble's address?"

She nodded. "Office and home are on Union Street."

"You two will need to palaver before the trial," Fargo told her. "I'll go fetch him when you're ready. Don't leave the hotel to go *any*where without me."

"That order apply to me, too?" Newt asked.

Fargo grinned, for he had noticed how Newt had been admiring the demimonde divas in their scarlet petticoats, eyes painted with dark kohl.

"You're a healthy, strapping lad," Fargo replied. "Just be careful to avoid the waterfront saloons—either your pocket gets picked, or you'll be shanghaied by some foreign sea captain."

"Man," Newt said, still watching the sporting gals stroll along the boardwalk. "In this town a fellow could go tripping the primrose path of dalliance all night long."

"Yeah," Fargo cracked, "and all day long he takes the mercury cure for clap."

Lindy cleared her throat.

"Sorry," Fargo told her, wiping the grin off his face.

"Skye?" Newt's voice was tense. "There's plenty of traffic, but have you noticed how most of the men lounging around are staring only at us?"

"Noticed it soon as we rode in. The staring I don't mind. But this is a city with a lot of guns going off, as you've noticed. It'd be too damn easy for some pond scum to toss lead at us. There *will* be trouble, so get set for it."

The weary travelers were able to rent adjoining rooms on the hotel's second floor. Fargo had suggested the Palace mainly because there was a decent livery nearby. It also offered the luxury, and safety, of bathtubs in each room instead of the usual out-back arrangement. Lindy, however, flew into transports at sight of all the satin pillows with lace ruffles as well as the stair railings of antique brass.

While Lindy and Newt were bathing and changing in their respective rooms, Fargo sat on a red plush chair between the doors.

When they finished, Fargo sent Newt to guard his sister

while the Trailsman washed up, then headed over to Union Street. There were more signs that San Francisco was changing: Fargo spotted more toppers and derbies than flap hats and sailors' caps. However, there were still plenty of lively saloons with girls topside, and oyster houses were still all the rage—shells littered the streets and crunched under Fargo's boots.

However, Fargo never lost sight of the various hardcases keeping an eye on him, some of them clearly Hounds, others apparently just local curs who licked any hand that tossed them rotgut money.

The Trailsman was passing a saloon called The Last Alibi, its doors thrown wide open to entice passersby. He glanced inside at the smoky interior and spotted several green baize poker tables, a few battered billiard tables sporting bullet holes and patched felts. Nothing special, just a run-of-the-mill watering hole.

"Well hello," Fargo said softly when he spotted a pretty faro dealer seated within a half circle of male bettors. The case tender called out each card like a circus barker.

The redheaded dealer, back, shoulders and much of her ivory-smooth breasts on display, noticed the tall, bearded man in buckskins watching her from the doorway. She sent him a low-lidded smile that caused a stirring in Fargo's trousers.

A boot scraped the boardwalk behind him. Fargo swiveled sideways to confront a man close to his own height, his bear-greased hair worn long and tied in back with a rawhide thong. The stink blowing off him made Fargo wince in disgust. No gun showed, but Fargo saw the telltale lump of a hideout gun under his thin sack coat.

"Mister," he greeted Fargo in a back-country twang, "you best check the brand before you drive another man's stock. Gretta is *my* woman."

Fargo laughed. "Only at gunpoint, chawbacon, would a beauty like that even be in the same room with the likes of you."

The hardcase's eyebrows arched, and his mouth set itself hard. Fargo gave him no time to take control of the situation, adding quickly, "Now me, I might have Gretta twice before lunch while you curry my horse. But she wouldn't let a drooling, toothless half-wit like you empty her piss pot."

Fargo was damned if these city thugs were going to run the show while *he* was on stage. Without preamble he set his heels hard, then sent a looping blow to the man's jaw. He staggered back, listed to one side, then thumped hard to the boardwalk as his knees came unhinged.

Fargo slipped a five-shot revolver from the still woozy man's inner pocket and flipped it casually out into the mud wallow called a street. He resumed his walk toward Union Street.

"Lead's gonna fly, you son of a bitch!" the thug shouted behind him, recovering awareness and spitting out blood.

Fargo pivoted on one boot heel and walked back. "I've noticed it generally does when I show up. Makes no sense, me being lovable and all. Except when I'm called a son of a bitch by some ugly pig-humper who smells like a jakes."

By now Wagner's louse was solidly on his feet again, one hand sliding inside his shirt. This time Fargo's fist exploded outward in a right cross, catching the bullyboy solidly on the lower jaw. Fargo's left hand reached in for the knife, a narrow-bladed dagger. It, too, went into the ooze of the street.

"Now," Fargo said in a tone that brooked no defiance, "has your butt-ugly face had enough?" He touched the grips of his Colt. "Or should we take this over to Telegraph Hill?"

The stranger, however, was staring at a puddle of blood on the boardwalk, his face ashen. A cracked yellow molar floated in it.

"Jesus Christ! You just knocked out my last goddamn jaw tooth, you son of a—uhh, I mean, *damn* you anyhow, mister."

"Blow in Gretta's ear for me, Romeo," Fargo dismissed the hapless fool, once again bearing toward Union Street.

"I certainly *will* introduce the crimes of Slade and McGuire into evidence," Tom Trumble assured Fargo. "If we can convince a jury those two well-known killers tried to murder Miss Helzer, it will be child's play to implicate Wagner. Everyone knows they worked for him, especially Slade. Preserving those bodies with your bullets in them was wise, Skye."

Trumble spoke with confident assurance, but to Fargo Lindy looked like a woman with serious misgivings.

"Mr. Trumble," she said, "I was reading *The Californian* just before you and Skye arrived. According to a front-page article, your county supervisor is a former inmate of Sing Sing?"

Trumble, who was leaning against the green marble mantel, looked pained. "As I mentioned to you during our correspondence, we still have a long row to hoe out here. But if we can bring Wagner to justice, the job gets easier. Law is based on precedent, and San Francisco desperately needs our first *legal* conviction."

Fargo was staying in motion, peeking out the windows of Lindy's room and occasionally listening at the door.

"All that makes sense," he remarked as he studied the teeming street below. "Unless you're Wagner."

Trumble's white-mustachioed face eased into a rueful smile. "Naturally. Wagner is a dictator, not a citizen. He's dead set against any law in San Francisco except gun law. *His* guns. And he can afford the best defense—he's a shake-down artist of the worst kind."

"What makes *him* the king?" Newt demanded. "Christ, one lowborn criminal running the city."

"Money makes a good bludgeon," Trumble said.

"So does a bludgeon," Fargo reminded him.

Trumble looked at Lindy. "I must be candid, Miss Helzer. We could *all* be sticking our heads in a noose, and I'm not being figurative. You can back out now—I'll just try the case on what I have."

Lindy, seated on the edge of a turkey-work bench, looked unsure.

"Just so you understand Mr. Trumble's point," Fargo told her, "he's suggesting there could be danger in the courtroom. Serious danger."

"Worse than we survived on the journey? Worse than assassins, Comanches, grizzly bears, howitzers, flash floods, dynamite?"

Fargo grinned. "Nope."

Lindy asked, "Will you be there with me in the courtroom?"

Fargo nodded.

"Then I'll testify," Lindy told Trumble.

"Thank God," he said, almost in a whisper. "With your testimony there's a strong chance Wagner gets gut-hooked. Without it, barely a weak chance. If we can prosecute Wagner, honest government will come to San Francisco sooner than later."

Fargo hoped so, but right now he had to be more practical than Trumble. "Gettin' back to the courtroom. Be any soldiers there?"

Trumble looked sheepish. "Since statehood we've had federal arms in the arsenal at Benicia. But when we finally formed a state guard, the local Vigilante Committee seized the boats bringing them to San Francisco. We have soldiers but no weapons for them."

"Un-*hunh*," Fargo said, showing nothing in his face to worry Lindy. There was indeed plenty to worry about, however. There were hundreds of hardened criminals prowling the streets out there, determined to murder Lindy and protect their criminal kingdom. And so far as a worried Fargo could tell, this wide-open boomtown was powerless to stop them.

15

Fargo was up most of the night of October 31, posted in front of Lindy's door. There was no commotion in the hotel, but just past midnight fire wagons raced to the courthouse on Sacramento Street. Trumble had told Fargo he expected an "accidental" fire and had posted roundsmen nearby. The arson fire was doused before much damage was done.

Even legal trials on the frontier were usually swift and streamlined. Trumble made his opening statement and presented the people's case in one day, reserving Lindy's appearance for the next morning. With the exception of a drunken mob gathering in the street outside, there was no trouble in the courthouse that first day.

"I *knew* it," a jubilant Trumble exclaimed that evening when they all met again in Lindy's room. "Did you see how serious the jury acted once Lindy came in and sat down? They don't know the details yet, but they know she's testifying, and it's obvious she's made a strong and positive impression on them."

"Plenty seem to know she's testifying," Fargo said, half his face hidden by a curtain as he watched the street below. "You saw that rabble outside the courthouse. Any chance you could get a couple honest roundsmen posted in the hotel lobby tonight?"

Trumble nodded. "Will do. But it's tomorrow I'm most worried about. Wagner can't let Lindy's story get out because he knows it will hang him. It's not impossible that Wagner's mob will attack the courthouse, and if they do we can't stop them."

The shadow of a smile twitched Fargo's lips. "Now, as to the mob . . . I might have an idea or two how to stop them. We have more to fear from attacks by killers who know what they're doing. Hell, that courtroom's got big windows on three walls."

"I'm armed," Trumble said, "and so is the judge and most of the jury even though they're not supposed to be. Frankly, so are most of the spectators in the courtroom."

"Including Wagner," Fargo said. "He wore his short iron openly."

"Thinks he's Wagner the Great," Trumble agreed. "He's all set to get elected mayor and run this place like he owns it."

Fargo glanced at Lindy, for whom all this was a terrifying ordeal that must be done for her sister's sake. Seeing Wagner today in court had unnerved her as it brought back horrible memories and images. Fargo had seen Wagner openly sneer at her.

"Wagner requires killing," Fargo told Trumble bluntly. "If the law can't do it, I can."

Next morning Lindy testified for over an hour, describing Wagner's rape and murder of her sister. Trumble deftly linked this to her description of Slade and McGuire's brutal attacks along the trail. Lindy wore a white shirtwaist and a black skirt, her hair in a chignon. She struck Fargo as very composed, very beautiful, and very convincing.

Fargo had permission to be present as Lindy's bodyguard, but not to prowl around the courtroom during the proceedings. He cast repeated, nervous glances at the windows. Every time he met Wagner's eyes, the arrogant bastard winked at him.

Fargo decided he was bluffing about feeling confident. The murdering rapist knew his hash was cooked, and there'd be a reckless play for his freedom coming up. That's all Wagner had left—it was too late to kill Lindy; her story was out.

Despite being primed for action, Fargo flinched hard when the window just to his right shattered inward. At the very first sound of glass breaking, the first to react were Wagner and his attorney, Beau Garrett. They dove through a hallway door and fled down a corridor. Obviously, they had planned this.

The third man to react was Fargo, and none too soon— a bundle of dynamite was throwing off a fountain of fizzling sparks only inches from his feet.

Fargo stayed frosty and relied on survival instincts honed over and over. Everybody around him was beginning to panic, trampling each other to reach the doors, but he instantly calculated the essential facts. There was no safe place to toss it, not with the street so crowded.

Cursing when he burned his fingertips, Fargo desperately pinched the main fuse and hoped he could break the crimping cap holding it to the primer. With barely a quarter inch of fuse left to burn, he pulled it loose.

Trumble had grabbed Lindy off the stand when the window broke. "Keep an eye on her, Tom!" Fargo called out as he raced toward the broken window, leaped, and shattered the rest of the pane as he landed in the grass outside, scattering several loiterers.

Expecting trouble, Fargo had paid a Mexican kid to hold the Ovaro in an alley beside the courthouse. Spotting a man racing down the street on a gray horse, obviously fleeing, Fargo vaulted into the saddle and gave chase.

Because of the trial, traffic was light at this hour. Still, Fargo had no plans to unlimber and fire, not in town. However, the thug changed all that when he began tossing snapshots wildly over his left shoulder. Fargo didn't fear being hit, but those wild slugs could fly into houses.

Fargo's Colt cleared leather, he snapped off a round, and the hurtling lead took off the top of the criminal's head like the lid of a cookie jar. Fargo spent only enough time to verify there was more dynamite in the dead man's saddle pannier, then raced back to the courtroom.

He was in for a shock when he climbed back through the window. Tom Trumble, bleeding from a wound in his arm, held a pistol aimed at Wagner—who in turn held the muzzle of a six-gun in Lindy's right ear, using her body as a shield.

"For once there were armed guards at the main entrance," Trumble muttered to Fargo. "Garrett's been shot dead. Wagner plugged me and got hold of Lindy. Now he figures she's his ticket to safety."

"Unless you want me to decorate the walls with this bitch's brains, Fargo," Wagner called out, "get around front and disarm those guards."

"Take it easy," Fargo said calmly. Lindy's eyes met Fargo's and he nodded imperceptibly. "I'll head out now and take care of it. You need anything else?"

Fargo was only speaking to hold Wagner's attention. Lindy's hand had slipped inside her shirtwaist.

"Yeah," Wagner snarled, swinging his gun toward Trumble, "I need that do-gooder cock chafer dead!"

The gun that went off, however, was the two-shot derringer Fargo had taken from Robles and given to Lindy. Her first shot only ruined Wagner's left eye, but the second hit a few inches higher and plowed a destructive furrow into his brain.

Fargo watched the criminal kingpin, the scourge of San Francisco, collapse to the floor like a sack of grain.

"Case closed, you son of a bitch," Fargo said softly.

"Here's all your pay, Skye," Lindy announced, counting out one hundred seventy dollars in gold cartwheels. "Talk about well earned."

"That's chicken feed to Skye," Newt teased. "He's sitting on two thousand dollars reward money. You think the city was going to demand proof he caught all four of those killers—not after what Skye did to bring Wagner and his toadies down."

The three of them were having dinner in the hotel lobby. Fargo had been having fun doing the mazy waltz with Lindy in her private room, but soon he'd have to leave. Reporters from the *Evening Bulletin* and other newspapers clamored for entrance to Fargo's room.

After all, he was the fearless man who had taken charge of the howling street mob after Wagner was killed. When Fargo appeared outside the courthouse, cracking the feared Judge Lash, the crowd scattered like chaff in the wind. But the Trailsman despised seeing his name in print and wanted only to lead an unchronicled existence—an elusive goal in the hero-hungry West.

"Given your attitude toward cities," Newt told Skye around a mouthful of steak, "I'm surprised you stayed here this long."

"The company's been excellent," Fargo said, grinning at Lindy. "Besides, I had a little promise to keep. I told Lofley and Coyote I'd be out there in the crowd, grinning, when they were hanged. Which happened yesterday."

"You were there?"

Fargo nodded. "Funny, though, I couldn't work up a grin. They needed hanging, all right, but there's nothing funny about killing any man."

Lindy said, "I'll never regret killing Wagner, never. But it wasn't as satisfying as I thought it might be."

"Never is," Fargo assured her. "So you two are headed back to Illinois?"

"Already booked on that Butterfield coach you mentioned," Lindy said. "All expenses paid by the city of San Francisco. And you—you'll be reporting for that railroad job down south of here?"

Fargo laughed. "Actually, I already sent them a telegram and told them I quit. Let some other poor dupe help them destroy the West. I've got plenty of money and a lively city to spend some of it in."

Not to mention, Fargo thought, a personal invitation to go visit a lovely faro dealer named Gretta.

"When it rains, it pours," he remarked with a sigh of contentment.

Lindy's big green eyes looked suddenly suspicious. "Is that a reference to the flood we survived?"

Fargo looked innocent as a newborn. "Sure. What else would it mean?"

LOOKING FORWARD!
The following is the opening
section of the next novel in the exciting
Trailsman series from Signet:

THE TRAILSMAN #293

OZARK BLOOD FEUD

The Ozark Mountains of Missouri, 1860—
where the chilly winds of winter
are no colder than the hearts of evil men.

The big man in buckskins and a sheepskin jacket tugged
his hat down tighter on his head and gritted his teeth
against the bite of the wind. His lake blue eyes squinted.
He was riding north, into the blustery gusts, and he didn't
like it.

Neither did the magnificent black-and-white stallion. The
Ovaro tossed his head and nickered as if to ask what they
were doing out in weather like this. He ought to be in a
warm stable somewhere, and his rider needed to be inside,
too, preferably with a hot meal in his belly.

That wasn't likely to happen anytime soon, Skye Fargo
told himself. He wasn't sure how far it was to the next
place where he could find shelter.

The late-afternoon sky was choked with thick gray clouds. The light of day was fading fast. The landscape was made even more dismal by the thickly wooded hills that loomed on both sides of the twisting road Fargo followed.

He had planned on reaching the settlement of Bear Creek by nightfall, but it looked like that wasn't going to happen. He would have to either push on after dark, or find a farm where he could spend the night.

The trail led through a little valley with a small stream at the bottom. As cold as it was, there would be ice on the edges of that creek by the next morning. The Ovaro's hooves rang on the crude bridge as it crossed. Fargo started up the slope on the northern side of the valley.

He reined in sharply. A frown creased his forehead as he stared up the road at the top of the hill.

Several figures were walking down the slope toward him. Fargo couldn't see them that well in the fading light, and they appeared shapeless because they were bundled up in heavy coats. He started to count. There were seven of them, and several of them were small.

Probably a family, thought Fargo as he rubbed the close-cropped dark beard on his jaw. The little ones would be kids. What were they doing out walking around on a frigid day like this?

He nudged the stallion into motion and headed up the hill toward the pilgrims. They didn't seem to notice him. They walked with their heads down and shoulders hunched, trying to stay warm, and since the wind was behind them, they evidently didn't hear the Ovaro's hoofbeats until Fargo had almost reached them.

Then the figure in the lead stopped short, yelled in alarm, and took a hurried step backward. He reached under his coat and brought out a gun. It was an old flintlock pistol, but at this range it could be as deadly as a more modern weapon.

"Don't come any closer! I'll shoot. I swear it!"

Fargo reined the Ovaro to a halt. The voice that had called the warning was high-pitched, probably not that of a woman but more likely a boy. The barrel of the old pistol shook, but whether that was from the cold or the nerves of the person holding it, Fargo didn't know. Probably some of both.

"Take it easy, son," Fargo said calmly. He didn't want to spook the boy into pulling the trigger. The youngster was trembling so much he would probably miss, but there was no point in taking chances. "I'm a friend."

"The hell you say." The boy probably hoped the profanity made him sound older. "We ain't got no friends in his neck of the woods."

"Well, I'm not an enemy, anyway," Fargo said. "Couldn't be, because I never saw you before."

Now that the boy was standing straighter and looking up at the man on the horse, Fargo could see his face better. It was pale and drawn, haggard with strain. The boy's nose was red and running from the cold. He looked scared out of his wits.

That didn't make him any less dangerous, of course. As long as he pointed that pistol at Fargo, he was a threat.

The others had come to a stop behind the boy and now huddled together in the road. One of them was a little taller than the boy with the gun. The rest were smaller.

"Calvin, be careful," said the taller one. Definitely a female voice this time, Fargo noted, and fairly young. "Don't shoot unless you have to."

"You don't have to tell me what to do, Junie," the boy snapped. "I got this under control."

He was so far from having the situation under control that it was sort of sad, but Fargo didn't point that out. Instead he asked, "Who are you folks, and why are you walking?"

"How else are you gonna get somewhere when you ain't go no wagon nor mules?" Calvin said. "We ain't lookin' for trouble, mister, so move aside and we'll be on our way."

"Where are you bound?"

"That's none of your business."

The sharp answer didn't surprise Fargo. Calvin wasn't the least bit friendly. Or maybe he was just so scared that he had put up a wall around him and wasn't going to let anybody else in.

The young woman spoke up again. "We're heading for Springfield."

Calvin jerked his head toward her. "Damn it, Junie, don't be tellin' this stranger anything! You know we can't trust nobody!"

Fargo could have urged the Ovaro forward while Calvin wasn't looking and ridden right over him. Fargo wasn't too worried anymore about the youngster being able to hit anything with that old horse pistol. He wasn't even convinced that the ancient weapon would actually fire.

But he stayed where he was, figuring he could do more good for these hapless pilgrims if he got them to trust him. He said, "I'm not looking for trouble, either. I'm bound for Jefferson City. Got a job waiting for me there."

"Jefferson City's a long way," Junie said.

"So's Springfield," Fargo pointed out. "Must be sixty, seventy miles from here." He had passed through the town several days earlier on his way north from Arkansas.

"Closer to eighty," the young woman said.

Calvin was getting frustrated. "Damn it, will you stop talkin' to this fella?" he burst out. "We got to keep movin'! You know that."

"You plan on walking all the way to Springfield?" Fargo asked.

Junie nodded. She had a scarf wrapped around her head. A few tendrils of blond hair strayed out from under it. "We don't have any choice. Like my brother said, we don't have a wagon or any mules to pull one."

So they were brother and sister. Fargo wondered if the smaller ones were their siblings, too. They watched Fargo with wide eyes. He could see now that some of them were wrapped up in threadbare blankets, rather than wearing coats.

"You can't walk that far in the middle of winter."

"Are you deaf, mister?" Calvin asked rudely. "Ain't nothin' else we can do."

"Don't you have a home?"

A couple of the little ones began to cry. When that happened, Fargo knew he had hit on something.

As Junie tried to comfort the ones who were crying and

get them to hush, Fargo said, "That's it, isn't it? You don't have a home."

"We got kinfolks in Springfield," Calvin said. "I reckon they'll take us in."

"But there's nowhere else you can go, so you have to walk halfway across Missouri in the dead of winter."

"We'll be fine." An edge of hysteria crept into Calvin's voice. Fargo guessed his pride wouldn't let him admit, even to himself, what a bad situation they were really in.

He nodded toward the little ones. "Are those your brothers and sisters?"

"You leave us alone," Calvin said thinly. "Don't you even think about takin' them away, or splittin' us up—"

"I'm not going to split anybody up," Fargo said. "But maybe I can help you—"

"No! There's nothin' anybody can do!"

One of the children suddenly gave a wail. "Calvin, I wanna go home!" she sobbed.

The boy spun toward her. "Shut up!" he cried raggedly. "Hush up that bawlin'!"

Junie put her arms around the smaller girl. "Calvin, stop it!" she scolded. "Hannah can't help it. She's worn-out and half-frozen like the rest of us."

She might be more than half-frozen before morning. Night was coming on soon, and the temperature would drop even more once darkness fell. And Fargo hadn't passed any place in the last ten miles where these children could take shelter.

This had gone on long enough. He swung down from the saddle.

Calvin must have heard him dismount. The boy whirled back around and started to bring the old pistol up. "I told you to leave us alone—" he began.

Fargo stepped forward swiftly, closed his hand around the barrel of the pistol, and yanked it out of Calvin's grasp. He moved past the angrily sputtering boy and handed the gun to Junie.

"I reckon I can trust *you* not to shoot me?"